Kittens in Trouble

Kittens in the Kitchen
Kitten in the Cold

LUCY DANIELS

Illustrations by Shelagh McNicholas

Hodder
Children's
Books

A division of Hachette Children's Books

This bind-up edition published in 2010 by Hodder Children's Books

**Special thanks to C. J. Hall, B.Vet.Med., M.R.C.V.S., for reviewing
the veterinary information contained in this book.**

Animal Ark is a trademark of Working Partners Limited
Text copyright © 1994 Working Partners Limited
Created by Working Partners Limited, London WC1X 9HH
Original series created by Ben M. Baglio
Illustrations copyright © 1994 Shelagh McNicholas

Kittens in the Kitchen published as a single volume in Great Britain in 1994
by Knight Books

The right of Lucy Daniels to be identified as the author of
this work has been asserted by her in accordance with the
Copyright, Designs and Patents Act 1988.

1

All rights reserved. Apart from any use permitted under
UK copyright law, this publication may only be reproduced,
stored or transmitted, in any form, or by any means with prior permission
in writing from the publishers or in the case of reprographic production in
accordance with the terms of licences issued by the Copyright Licensing Agency
and may not be otherwise circulated in any form of binding or cover other than
that in which it is published and without a similar condition
being imposed on the subsequent purchaser.

All characters in this publication are fictitious and any resemblance to real
persons, living or dead, is purely coincidental.

A Catalogue record for this book is available from the British Library

ISBN 978 1 444 90271 6

Typeset in Baskerville by Avon DataSet Ltd,
Bidford-on-Avon, Warwickshire

Printed and bound in Great Britain by CPI Bookmarque, Croydon

The paper and board used in this paperback by Hodder Children's
Books are natural recyclable products made from wood grown in
sustainable forests. The manufacturing processes conform to the
environmental regulations of the country of origin.

Hodder Children's Books
a division of Hachette Children's Books
338 Euston Road
London NW1 3BH
www.hachette.co.uk

Kittens in the Kitchen

To Jenny Oldfield, who loves animals,
and to Peter and Benjamin,
the kittens in my kitchen

One

'Mandy, you're very keen on school all of a sudden,' Mr Hope said. He watched her stuff old newspapers into her schoolbag. She flung on her school jacket, flicked a brush through her dark blonde hair and snatched a mouthful of toast. 'It's only ten to eight. Are you sure you're OK?'

'Very funny!' Mandy said. 'Of course I'm OK. It's just a special day, that's all.' She'd fed her rabbits and done her morning chores at Animal Ark. Simon, the nurse, had come in to take over care of the animals and do temperatures and medicines. Now she was free to go.

'School trip?' Mr Hope took a guess as Mandy unlocked her bicycle padlock and put on her crash-helmet. He got no reply. 'New boyfriend?'

'Ha, ha!' Mandy said. 'No time now, Dad. I'll tell you later.' She set off up the front drive, her long legs pedalling like mad. She waved at her mother.

'What's the rush?' Mrs Hope wound down her car window.

But Mandy had already sped by, under the wooden sign, 'Animal Ark, Veterinary Surgeon'. She took one look back at the old stone cottage with its modern vets' extension to the rear, then she pedalled hard again. Her heavy schoolbag dragged across her shoulder.

'She's up to something,' Mandy heard Mrs Hope say. 'She's got that determined look on her face.'

Mandy knew they wouldn't have a clue what she wanted with the old newspapers. But she ignored them and charged up the lane towards Welford village. She'd keep her mystery until evening, after Mrs Hope came back from her round of visits to the sick cats, dogs, goats and hamsters that made up the busy practice of

Animal Ark. She gave her mum and dad one last wave before she turned out on to the road. 'See you later!' she yelled.

'This is it! This is the big day!' Mandy greeted her friend, James Hunter. As usual, his straight brown hair flopped on to his forehead, and his glasses sat halfway down his nose.

'Hi,' he said. 'Do you realise I've dragged myself out of bed half an hour early to meet up with you outside this rotten post office!' He was breathless from pedalling. 'My dad nearly dropped dead with shock!'

'Come on!' Mandy said, ignoring his protests, 'Let's go and see!'

Mandy and James cycled out of Welford on the two mile stretch into Walton. Past all the sleepy cottages and wide awake farms with their collie dogs at the gate, she never once stopped chattering.

'It's going to be today, I know it!' She had a feeling about these things. James nodded and panted to keep up. 'I'm so excited, I can hardly wait!' The ground sped by under their wheels. 'She's been looking for a warm dry place, and that's always a sign! Anyway, she refused her food yesterday.' James nodded again in agreement. 'I did see her in the caretaker's porch yesterday after school, behind the stack of logs. She's a very clever cat!'

They pedalled down the final hill. Mandy's short hair blew back in the wind. The new bungalows of Walton greeted them, spick and span. Walton Moor School lay behind these new houses; another new building which backed on to open countryside. Mandy and James rode through the gateway into the deserted playground.

Mr Williams, the caretaker, strode through the grounds, setting out parking cones for the dustbin lorry. It was Thursday, bin day. 'Morning!' Mandy called, with James running to catch up. But Mr Williams was a man of few words. He ignored her greeting.

'Shh, now!' Mandy warned James. They'd left their bikes locked up in the shed, and came up behind the caretaker's house. 'We don't want to disturb her.' Carefully they peered over the beech hedge, neatly trimmed by Mr Williams. They scanned his pink rose bushes and the porch at the back of his house.

'Mandy,' James dared to whisper, 'does

Mr Williams know about this?' He was cleaning his glasses on his school jumper. 'I mean, what will he say if he finds us snooping about on his porch?'

'He won't mind,' Mandy whispered back. How could anyone mind about animals? 'Mrs Williams sometimes puts out food. I expect that's why Walton has chosen their porch to have her babies in!' Mandy's face shone with excitement.

'Walton?' James didn't realise the cat had a name. It was small, black and white and rather ordinary. As far as he knew, it was a stray. But then Mandy had kept details about the cat pretty much to herself up till now.

'I named her after the school,' Mandy said. 'According to Mrs Williams, she just turned up on the main doorstep one night, dumped inside a plastic bag, with tiny airholes to breathe through. Can you believe it? People can be so cruel!'

Mandy could feel the prick of tears in her eyes even now. 'She was only a young cat and someone just dumped her!' She sniffed and tried to pull herself together. 'She would've died if I hadn't come along early next morning and gone to the staffroom for some milk for her. She was really neglected. I had to feed her up.' She squared her shoulders. 'Anyway, that was six weeks ago. She's the school cat now, only a sort of half stray. So it's up to us to look after her!'

With that, Mandy eased open the back gate into the Williams's garden. 'Walton! Walton!' she coaxed, bending low and looking under the stilted porch into the dark space there. James peered up on to the porch itself, behind the stack of logs. No cat.

'Walton!' Mandy called, a bit more loudly.

A black and white shape trotted across the long shadows of the lawn, and over the flower-bed; a round, heavy shape, nearly as wide as she was long, with a low belly. James spotted her first. 'Mandy, look!' he said.

Mandy breathed a sigh. They'd got here in time. 'Hello, Walton,' she said. 'Here's a nice, comfy place for you to give birth to your lovely kittens, see!' She climbed the porch steps. The cat followed. Mandy delved into her bag and drew out the old newspapers. She showed them to Walton and let her sniff them. 'See, nice and warm and dry!'

Then she and James banked up some of the logs to make a sort of den for Walton. They lined it with the newspapers, carefully overlapping them in thick layers. 'See!' Mandy said again.

Walton brushed against Mandy's bare legs. She tilted her head up towards the special bed of logs and newspapers. Her delicate nose and whiskers seemed to approve, for she climbed, slow and heavy, up on to the ledge.

'It's in the sun, nice and warm,' James said. 'Good idea!' He grinned at Mandy then blushed. In the distance, the morning bell sounded. 'Was that the bell?' he asked clumsily. Then he shot off for registration before Mandy could reply.

'You hear that, Walton?' Mandy said. 'That's the bell. I have to go.' But she felt the strong pull that the cat had over her. Perhaps it was because she, Mandy Hope, aged thirteen, of Animal Ark, Welford, Yorkshire, was very like Walton, the school cat. They were both adopted. Her own parents had died in a car crash, too early for her to remember them, and Adam and Emily Hope had taken her in. Now she would do the same for Walton.

Softly she stroked the cat, then she caught hold of herself. 'I'll stop fussing now and leave you to cope.' She knew animals liked privacy at this time. 'No one will bother you, and I'll be back later to see how you've got on.' Quietly she backed down from the porch, then quickly she cut across the garden, through the gate and over the tarmac of the playground. The second bell had gone.

Mr Williams, in his padded green waistcoat, his old corduroy trousers and his big laced boots, crossed paths with Mandy as she ran into school through the main door. As usual, he only grunted, head down and grumpy. Mandy thought it was best not to say anything to him about Walton and her arrangements for the birth. Leave it till later. Even Mr Williams's heart would melt once he saw Walton's kittens nestling on his back porch!

Mandy rushed into lessons. She tried, and failed, to concentrate all the way through maths, geography and English.

At half past three James was waiting for Mandy at the lockers. 'Ready?' he asked. Like Mandy, animals were the most important thing in James's life.

Dodging the crowds, they sprinted together up the slope to the caretaker's house. Mandy could hardly breathe for excitement. This was Walton's big day!

'Walton!' Mandy called, easing the gate, crossing the lawn. They turned the corner up on to the porch. Mandy half closed her eyes. There Walton would be, tucked up in her newspaper bed, shielding her new kittens! She couldn't wait!

She opened her eyes. The bed was empty! Clean and dry and quite empty. Mandy looked at James. They felt the bottom of the world fall out.

'Where is she?' James gasped.

Mandy shook her head. 'It's today. I'm sure it's today.' She couldn't understand it. She'd seen enough cats giving birth to kittens at Animal Ark to know just how they looked when the great day came. Mandy and James stood on the porch, confused and alarmed.'

'Listen!' Mandy said. The Williamses' back door stood open in the afternoon sunshine, and Mandy was sure she'd picked up a sound from inside. A tiny, high-pitched squeaking sound!

James stared at her. 'What is it?'

Mandy stepped across the kitchen threshold. 'Mr Williams?' she whispered. 'Mrs Williams?'

The kitchen was neat and clean, scrubbed to perfection. Its lace curtains shone pure white. Its black and white tiles looked like an advertisement for floor cleaner. But it was empty. The squeaking noise was slightly louder. 'In here!' Mandy said.

They tiptoed into the empty room.

'It's still very muffled,' James said. He looked inside cupboards, trying to find the noise.

They looked under shelves, behind the vegetable rack, but still the noise escaped them.

'Walton!' Mandy called gently.

But Walton, wherever she was, didn't want company. Only the muffled, faint squeaking continued. Mandy followed it until she finally tracked it down.

There was a linen basket in the corner of the kitchen, by the washing-machine. It was an old-fashioned straw one with a lid. Mandy put her ear to it. The squeaking came from inside!

Gingerly she lifted the lid. It was dark and warm in there. The high-pitched noise rose to a wailing chorus. Mandy adjusted her eyes to the darkness and peered inside. She saw the black and white patches of Walton's fur, she saw the cat's eyes glint as she looked up. Obligingly, Walton lifted a paw and shifted sideways. 'Look!' she seemed to be saying, 'Four perfect kittens!'

Mandy could just make them out; four tiny curled up things, grey and blind. Skinny, helpless creatures. She thought they were the most beautiful things she'd ever seen!

'Aren't they wonderful!' Mandy breathed, as James came to look over her shoulder.

He saw their blunt little faces and blind eyes. 'Ye-es,' he said. He clearly needed more time to get used to them.

'Oh, but they are!' Mandy cooed. She touched Walton gently under the chin. 'Clever girl!' she said. The kittens squeaked louder in protest at the light and the cooler air. Mandy gave in and replaced the laundry basket lid.

And then their luck ran out. Someone crossed the porch and filled the kitchen doorway. He was tall, bulky, and his feet made a noise across the wooden floor of the porch. 'Amy?' he called. He paused, wiped his feet, then stepped into the kitchen.

'Mr Williams! Um, hello!' Mandy said feebly. James stood alongside her, straightening his school tie, trying to look braver than he felt.

'What the heck!' Williams bellowed with shock. 'Amy! Where are you? What the heck!' he said again.

His wife came pottering through from the front room. She was slightly deaf, slightly short-sighted. 'Don't shout, Eric,' she sighed. 'I can hear perfectly well without you having to shout!'

'Oh, can you?' her husband fumed. 'I expect you heard these two prowling around in here perfectly well, too!'

Mrs Williams sighed again. 'Sit down all of you,' she said. 'Everybody sit down while I make us a cup of tea!' It was clearly her cure for everything.

Mandy and James sat down as they were told, as far away from Mr Williams as possible, while his wife made the tea. 'Well!' he said over and over. 'Can't a man even call his house his own any more?'

'Oh, shush, Eric!' his wife said, giving him his favourite mug and a Rich Tea biscuit. 'Just give them a chance to explain!' She was little and skinny, half his size, but Mandy and James could see who was boss. 'Well, then,' Mrs Williams smiled sweetly at Mandy. 'I'm sure there's a perfectly good explanation!'

'There is,' Mandy agreed. She looked wildly at James for help.

'The cat's had kittens!' James blurted out.

'In your laundry basket,' Mandy finished off.

'What!' Mr Williams shot to his feet. He backed off into a corner.

'Wait!' Mrs Williams went to investigate. She

lifted the basket lid and peered inside. 'It has,' she confirmed calmly. 'It's had kittens all right.'

'On my best shirts!' Mr Williams stammered. 'It's had kittens on my best shirts!'

'Calm down, Eric!' Mrs Williams shook her head. 'It's only a stray cat!'

'Only!' The caretaker rolled his eyes in helpless anger.

'She won't do any harm,' Mandy broke in. 'They're very clean animals. She won't leave any mess!' She tried to reason with him. 'If you just leave her and the kittens in peace in there for a few days, they'll soon be on their feet. Then you can make them a better place; a cardboard box, for instance. Just line it with newspaper and put it out on the porch. That should be fine!'

'A few days!' Mr Williams repeated. His face seemed to be stuck. His mouth had dropped open, his eyes were bulging.

Mrs Williams took Mandy and James to one side. She shook her head. 'It's no use. He can't stand them.'

Mandy was slow to catch on. 'Can't stand what?' Only now was she beginning to sense there was a problem.

'Cats. He can't stand them. They set his nerves on edge.'

Mandy breathed in deeply. How could people hate cats?

'He says they dig up his garden. He can't abide them.' Mrs Williams sounded sorry, but she sounded as if they'd just have to understand. Her husband was stubborn as a mule over cats. She turned and started clearing away the tea things.

'Just a few days!' Mandy said, dashing from one to the other. 'We can't move them for a few days in case the mother decides to abandon the kittens. She might do if they get moved. Please let her stay where she is!' She felt breathless with fright, but she tried not to show it.

'Stay? In my linen basket!' Mr Williams snorted. 'On my best shirts!' He tossed his head. 'A load of smelly cats!'

'They're not—' Mandy interrupted, but James stopped her. He had a better idea of when to answer back than Mandy.

'Not likely!' Mr Williams headed straight at Mandy and James to shoo them out of his kitchen. 'Go on, you two. Look sharp! I shan't warn you again!'

Mandy and James backed off towards the door. Mr Williams towered over them. 'Please!' Mandy pleaded. She felt sick at heart.

'No!' Mr Williams thundered. 'They've got to go!' He glanced at his wife. 'And there's no use you looking like that, Amy, so you can just pipe down! I'm saying no and I mean no!' He looked down at Mandy's terrified face. 'I'm telling you once and for all, I'm not having them kittens in my kitchen!'

Two

Mr Williams said his final word then stormed out of the room. Tears sprang to Mandy's eyes. She looked in desperation at Mrs Williams.

The old woman raised her eyebrows and rolled her eyes. She patted her neat grey hair. 'Just give him a minute to cool down,' she said. She lifted the linen basket lid to take a peek for herself. 'My, my,' she murmured.

'He can't mean it,' Mandy said to James, who was trying to drag her out of the kitchen on to the back porch. 'He can't just sentence four perfectly harmless kittens to death, can he? It isn't fair!'

James shook his head and kept on pulling. 'Come on, we'd better go!'

'Mrs Williams!' Mandy pleaded.

The caretaker's wife carefully washed up the rose-patterned teacups. She put them away in a high, glass-fronted cupboard. 'I'm saying nothing,' she said steadily.

Mandy shook herself free of James. 'But it isn't fair, is it? I mean, what have those poor little kittens ever done to anybody? They deserve a chance to live, just like anyone else! You can't just chuck them away because they happen to have been born in an unusual place!'

'On top of my husband's best shirts,' Mrs Williams reminded her. 'My Eric's very particular about his shirts.' She turned to face Mandy, who was head and shoulders taller, but thin as a piece of string. 'Anyhow, whoever said life was fair?'

'But if he moves them, they'll die! Walton will abandon them!' Again the tears pricked her eyelids.

Mrs Williams stared up at her. 'Walton?' She folded her arms and kept her gaze steady.

'The mother cat. I've called her Walton after the school. I wanted her to sound as if she belonged somewhere! As if she was looked after, and had a home, and somebody who cared!' Mandy rushed on.

The tears were rolling down her cheeks now. They ran with a salty taste into her mouth. She remembered the half-starved cat being dumped in the school doorway. She thought of herself. What would have happened to her if Emily and Adam Hope hadn't taken her in and cared for her when she was tiny?

'Mandy!' James whispered. 'Don't cry. You see worse things than this at the Ark every day of the week, remember.'

'No, let her alone,' Mrs Williams said thoughtfully. 'She's right. They deserve a chance.' She took Mandy by the hand and sat her down at the table. Late afternoon sun filtered in through the white net curtains. 'But for goodness sake, dry your eyes, young woman. I can hear my Eric coming back across the yard, and he can't abide waterworks!' She pulled a clean handkerchief out of her apron pocket and handed it to Mandy. 'Quick, blow your nose!'

'Will you help us?' Mandy whispered. The caretaker's big boots tramped up the steps and across the porch. 'If you let the kittens stay, I'll come here every day, twice a day, to help look after them! I'll—'

'Shush!' Mrs Williams warned. Her husband hung his cap on the door peg. She stood up and leaned forward evenly, with clenched fists down on the table.

'What the—!' Mr Williams's face darkened as he caught sight of Mandy and James. 'I thought I'd told you to clear off! What's the matter, are you deaf?'

'Now, Eric,' Mrs Williams began steadily.

'Don't you "now, Eric" me!'

'Now, Eric!' she insisted. 'This young girl has been explaining to me again about these kittens being moved. It seems the mother won't have any more to do with them if we interfere. They've to be left alone.'

A loud miaow of agreement from inside the basket backed up the end of Mrs Williams's firm speech. Thin squeaks followed after in a kind of chorus. Mr Williams paced up and down the kitchen.

'Stand still, Eric, and listen!' Hands on hips, the tiny woman in the flowery apron confronted her heavyweight husband. 'Where's the harm in it? You've a drawer full of shirts up those stairs, most of them hardly worn. There's even one still in its packet, pins and all. The one that your sister gave you last Christmas!' She eyed him sternly.

'You know I don't like shirts straight from the wrapping,' he grumbled. 'They're stiff and they itch!'

'I'll wash it specially.' She didn't flinch. 'Then you can wear it this Sunday to chapel, all right?'

Mandy held her breath. She had the good sense not to interfere in this argument, even though the little wailing sound from inside the basket was tugging at her heartstrings. James still stood sentry by the door, ready to scarper.

Mr Williams pointed an accusing finger at the basket. 'My best blue shirt! My favourite!' he reminded her angrily. But it was the last squib of resistance. He knew when he was beaten.

'Now, Eric, it won't come to any harm. This young girl knows all about animals, don't you?'

Mandy nodded and gasped. 'My mum and dad are both vets. In Welford, at Animal Ark!'

Mrs Williams nodded too. 'See, she's a good girl. She's promising to come in here twice a day to help look after those poor wee things. They won't get under your feet. They'll just stay in there nice and cosy while Walton tends them.'

'Walton?' Mr Williams interrupted, looking curiously at Mandy.

'The mother cat,' Mrs Williams said, steady as ever.

'Daft name for a cat,' he grumbled, but he was definitely weakening.

'Well?' the fierce little woman demanded.

'Well . . .' He scratched his lined forehead with broad, workworn fingers.

'Right, that's settled then!' she said, like snapping a suitcase shut. 'The girl will come in here each day until the kittens can begin to fend for themselves.'

Mr Williams grunted.

'That means yes,' she reported to Mandy and James.

Mandy jumped up from the table, able to breathe at last. 'Oh, thank you!' she said in a rush. 'I'll go straight off and get some food and extra vitamins and things for Walton. I'll be back as soon as I can. Walton will need lots of looking after, being such a small cat, and we may have to help her feed her kittens. I'll bring milk and a dropper just in case. She won't have that much milk herself, and four is a lot for her to feed, especially being so run down when she was a stray! We'll need to—'

'Whoa, hold your horses!' Mr Williams backed off against the wall. 'Not so fast.' He turned to James. 'Now listen, lad, maybe I can talk sense to you!'

James stood to attention, ready to listen.

'Man to man, I'm telling you straight, mind. My wife Amy is too soft-hearted by far. Everyone knows that. And I've agreed to let those dratted kittens stay put on top of my shirts because of her. I don't like it, but I want a quiet life. And when my wife makes up her mind about something, I generally give in.'

Mrs Williams smiled at Mandy, her hands clasped meekly in front of her.

'But,' said Mr Williams, 'I just want to give your girlfriend here a word of warning.'

Mandy saw James's face colour up at the word 'girlfriend'. But Mr Williams thundered on.

'Now, I'm a mild-mannered chap, but before

you both go running off for food and vitamins and whatever else, I want to make it clear that I won't put up with these smelly things camping out on my best shirts for a day longer than necessary, is that clear?'

James nodded. Mandy moved over to the door to stand beside him. They watched Mr Williams's face take on the old angry look. 'Quiet life or not, I'll give you just one week,' he warned. 'And that'll be your lot! After that, it's the end for the nasty little creatures!'

Mandy felt her heart go thump. She felt the blood drain from her face. 'What do you mean?'

'I mean what I say. I'm giving you seven days. Find good homes for those kittens within the week, or else!' He stood with his feet planted wide apart, his face like a storm.

'Or else what?' Mandy gasped.

'Or else I'll deal with them myself!' He turned and stamped out of the kitchen, slamming the door after him.

James and Mandy flew back home on their bikes, up and down the hills to Welford. At the back of her mind hammered the horrible phrase, 'deal with them myself'. Meaning what? Pictures of kittens drowning, hanging, being dumped in a sack by the side of a motorway flashed through her head.

She yelled goodbye to James at the Fox and Goose crossroads and pelted on up the track to Animal Ark. When she arrived, she threw down her bike in the backyard and rushed straight into the surgery.

'Mum!' she called. She dashed past Jean Knox in Reception, who was busy signing out Miss Martin's Yorkshire terrier, Snap.

Jean looked up and smiled. 'She's in the unit,' she said, but the door was already swinging shut.

'Mum!' Mandy slowed herself down and lowered her voice so as not to disturb the animals in their rows of cages and kennels.

'Hi, Mandy, over here!' Mrs Hope called. She had a blue-grey Persian cat up on the treatment table and was carefully feeling behind his left ear. She gave the cat a kindly stroke and popped him back in his basket. 'You're just about ready for home,' she promised. She turned to Mandy. 'Now, what's all the drama?'

Her mum stood there in her white coat. She

wore her long red hair tied back as usual, but it was always escaping. With her big green eyes and friendly face, Mrs Hope had the knack of calming Mandy down. 'The school cat's had four kittens,' she reported.

'Ah!' Mrs Hope smiled. 'That explains the newspapers. Good bedding for a birth. Did you get there on time?'

'Yes, but she didn't like the place on the porch that we'd sorted out for her.' Mandy fiddled with the catch on the Persian's basket.

'No. They often don't.' Mrs Hope hooked her thumbs in her coat pockets. 'So?'

'So she gave birth in the caretaker's kitchen instead.'

'And?'

'And Mr Williams, the caretaker, hates cats!' Mandy looked at her mother with her wide blue eyes.

'Ah!' Mrs Hope settled back against the treatment table. Mr Hope came out of one of the treatment rooms to join them.

'Mu-um!' Mandy began to plead. 'He's given us a week. We've got to find homes for four kittens in a week. Otherwise he's threatening to take them off somewhere and put them down!'

Mrs Hope looked at her husband. 'Hmm.'

'It's not fair!' Mandy exploded. 'He cares more about his stupid shirts than about the lives of four innocent animals! How can anyone be so mean?'

'Calm down, Mandy,' Mr Hope said. He was rubbing his beard thoughtfully. 'What's this about shirts?'

Mandy explained. 'Anyway, the kittens will be up and about in a few days, then it'll be OK to move them out of the stupid basket. Then he can have his rotten shirts back!'

'Mandy!' her mum warned. 'Don't be rude. Some people just don't like cats and you have to accept that.' She lifted the cat basket and began to head for Reception.

Mandy realised that her chance was slipping by. 'Mum,' she said, 'can I take some milk and some vitamins back over there tonight?' She knew from watching her parents at work in Animal Ark what help Walton would need to feed the kittens.

'Of course,' Mrs Hope nodded. She was already on her way out.

'And, Dad, can we take the kittens in here at

the end of the week? Please!' Mandy sidled up to him.

'Ah!' Mr Hope put an arm round her shoulder. He knew Mrs Hope was still listening. 'Now, Mandy, you know our rules about that.'

'I know, Dad, but this is different!' Mr Williams was going to kill the poor little things if she couldn't find them homes!

'We don't take in strays, you know that. We're not a charity, remember. We're vets.' Mandy guessed that it was a rule he might have bent a little. But his wife had a very firm business head. She came back towards them.

'The answer's got to be no, Mandy.' Mrs Hope was kind but firm. She put the cat basket down and spoke gently. 'Listen, the caretaker has already done you a favour and given you a week, hasn't he?'

Mandy hung her head and nodded miserably. 'It would only be for a while, Mum. We'd only have to have them for a while until Walton's finished feeding.'

'Then what, eh?' Mrs Hope glanced at her husband to check. 'That's right, isn't it, Adam? We can't suddenly change our rule about strays. We'd be overrun with them in no time. You've

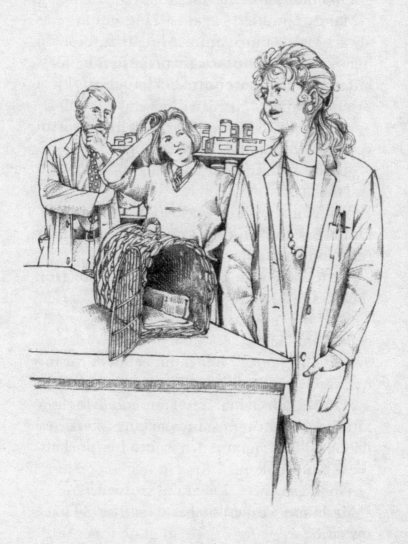

got to understand that, Mandy.'

Mandy nodded again. Her mum was always right, but it hurt a lot to agree with her sometimes. She thought of the four helpless kittens being carefully licked clean by a proud Walton.

'Now, listen,' Mr Hope said in his cheerful voice. 'Cheer up, this is a challenge!'

Mandy sniffed and looked up. 'How do you mean?'

'You've got a whole week; look at it that way! One week to find four good homes for four furry bundles of fun. You can do it!'

She looked up at his lopsided, cheerful grin. 'I can,' she agreed. 'Or rather, *we* can!'

'We?' her mum asked.

'Me and James.'

'You and James!' her mum echoed, raising her eyebrows. 'Well, then!'

Mandy ignored her. 'Yes! Four homes for four kittens!' Mandy began packing sterilised droppers and vitamin drops into her pockets. 'Easy. No problem!'

'Good girl,' Mrs Hope said, satisfied.

Mr Hope winked at his daughter. 'That's my girl!'

Mandy was dashing about, back to normal. 'I'll sort this out, just you wait!' She was out through Reception, grinning at Jean, stroking two black Labradors and a hamster, jumping on her bike and pedalling up the drive before her parents had time to draw breath.

Back at school, Mrs Williams opened the kitchen door to her and watched as Mandy gently lifted the lid of the laundry basket.

'Hello, Walton,' Mandy coaxed. Inside the basket it was warm and dark. The cat purred up at her. 'Come on, come and have some food!' She picked up the warm, soft cat and cradled her. The four kittens wailed miserably. 'Sorry, but mother cats need looking after too!' Mandy said as she closed the lid.

'There!' Mandy said as she set out milk and food on the kitchen floor for Walton. The cat arched her black and white back and rubbed against Mandy's legs. Then she settled quickly and daintily to her supper.

'Come and look!' Mandy whispered to Mrs Williams. 'Walton won't mind.' Walton raised her head briefly as Mandy lifted the basket lid once more, then carried on lapping milk. They peered together into the dark nest. Clean and dry, the four kittens nestled on Mr Williams's best blue shirt; blind and helpless, but quiet now, and snuggled against one another.

'Oh, my!' Mrs Williams shook her head. 'They look like drowned rats!'

'No, they don't. They're beautiful!' Mandy whispered. 'Look!'

'Well, at any rate they all look the same to me, all grey and furry and curled up like that.'

'No, they don't. They're very different; can't you see?' And Mandy promptly decided to give them names. She picked them up, one at a time. 'This one's Smoky, and this one's Patch.' She looked carefully at the two remaining kittens, then grinned. 'And this one's Amy. And this one's Eric!'

'Oh!' Mrs Williams stood back, slightly shocked, then pleased in spite of herself. 'Are you sure? I mean, I don't know what my husband will say!' She tut-tutted and smoothed her apron.

Mandy smiled and stood up as Walton finished her meal.

The cat leapt up on to the basket, back on duty. She sprang down into the dark well, ready to let the kittens suckle. 'I think we'll let her manage for now.' She put the lid back on, testing it to make sure the cat could push it off easily by herself. 'Maybe tomorrow we'll start giving the kittens extra.'

'Hmm.' Mrs Williams nodded. 'What time will you be back in the morning then?'

'About eight o'clock. Before school starts.'

The caretaker's wife showed her out. 'Mind you don't forget!'

'No way!' Mandy waved, picked up her bike and set off for home.

The sun was setting over the moor as she rode up out of Walton, past the new bungalows out on to the open road. The sky was pure red, the horizon dark brown. Mandy felt the wind. She was pleased with the day, happy that Walton had had such a good birth. She'd be a wonderful mother, even though she was so young herself.

Then Mandy's heart jolted. Smoky and Patch, Amy and Eric were all snuggled up for the night. There was a new world waiting outside for them, a big and dangerous place. Just now they were asleep. But Mandy tensed against the handlebars as she took the final curve down the hill into Welford. Her face frowned. She had a week to find four homes. Mr Williams's threat lurched out of the lengthening shadows like a giant from a fairy tale. 'Find good homes for them kittens within the week. Or else I'll deal with them myself!' he roared. Mandy knew he wouldn't relent. He meant what he said. A death sentence hung over the poor little kittens, and only she could save them!

Three

Mr Hope glanced up from the television as Mandy wandered in. The sitting-room was low, with wooden beams, a big stone inglenook fireplace and cosy red-patterned carpets on the old stone floor. It was a cold evening and a log fire crackled. 'Got any homework?' he asked.

'I've already done it.' Mandy flicked through a copy of *The Dalesman*. She was frowning and restless.

Mr Hope looked at her again. 'Why not take that back to your gran's?' he suggested.

Mandy nodded. She was thinking, thinking; what to do to find homes for those kittens? But she picked up the little magazine and drifted off down the hallway.

'Where are you off to?' her mum asked as she came in through the front door. She'd just got back from her yoga class, relaxed and smiling as usual.

'I have to clean out the rabbit hutch, then I'm off to Gran and Grandad's,' Mandy said absent-mindedly. She waved the magazine, still deep in thought.

'Say hello from me!' Mrs Hope shouted, but she got no answer.

Mandy let Flopsy, Mopsy and Cottontail out into the run in the back garden while she cleaned out their hutch and laid down fresh straw. Satisfied that their water was clean and that they were safely bedded down for the night, she set off up the lane to her grandparents' cottage.

In the cool evening light the mass of white lilacs in her grandad's garden gave off a strong, sweet scent. Even at this late hour he would be out in his greenhouse, pottering. 'Hi, Grandad!' she said with a wave. She stood to wait for him by the new camper van sitting proudly in their side drive.

'Hello, love!' His face lit up and he came out to greet her. He slid the greenhouse door closed. 'Come in, come in. Your grandma's inside writing letters.'

He showed her in through the kitchen into the cosy back room. The lamps cast a yellow glow and the flowered curtains were closed. 'Hello!' Mandy's grandmother shone her a wide smile. 'Guess what I'm doing.'

Mandy sat down opposite her at the table. 'Writing a letter!' She loved visiting her grandparents. Even when she felt down, like now, somehow they cheered her up.

'Not just any old letter!' her grandmother announced. 'This one is special. This one is to the Prime Minister!'

'Oh!' Mandy tried not to sound too surprised. She was used to her gran knitting impossible cardigan patterns and making kilos of rhubarb and ginger jam, not writing letters to prime ministers. 'What is it about?' she asked.

'It's about our post office. There's nasty rumours in the village that they want to close it down. Mr McFarlane told me about it when I went in to collect our pension earlier today.'

'Why do they want to close it?' Mandy couldn't imagine life in Welford without McFarlane's post office. She'd bought sherbet in there ever since she was tiny; she'd bought water-pistols, bubble-gum, comics, and sometimes soap powder for her mum when they ran out. When she'd forgotten James's birthday last month, she'd popped down to McFarlane's for a flowered card with a terrible verse:

> Here's a birthday treat
> For someone very sweet.
> Kind thoughts and wishes too
> For a friend as nice as you!

Gran raised her glasses on to her forehead. 'They say it's too dear to run. Too dear, I ask you! Honestly, they don't know what they're talking about! We have to stop them!'

'So Dorothy's writing to the Prime Minister. Always go to the top is what I say,' Mandy's grandad said. 'On her best notepaper of course!' He winked and handed her a glass of homemade lemonade.

'On my official notepaper. I'm writing as chairperson of Welford Women's Institute!'

Mandy looked impressed. Even the Prime Minister would have to listen to her grandmother when she was on her high horse. 'They won't close the post office,' she said. 'Not after they've read your letter!'

They all chuckled. 'You've spoilt my flow,' her grandmother said. She put pen and paper to one side. She looked at Mandy's fidgety hands. 'Anyway, you've got something on your mind, I can tell.'

Mandy didn't need a second invitation. The story of Walton and her kittens poured out; how she was the school cat, but Mandy felt she must take charge. How Mr Williams had no heart at all. How she, Mandy, had to find homes for the kittens. Her grandparents nodded, tutted and nodded in all the right places. Mandy paused at the critical point and took a deep breath. 'Gran,' she said, trying to sound very reasonable, 'I've been thinking.'

'Yes?' Her grandmother gave her a sideways look.

'Well, I've been thinking that a cat would be the perfect thing for you here in the cottage. I mean, it's a bit lonely this far up the lane and you hardly see any neighbours, and a cat is really good company for . . .' She faltered and blushed.

'For old people?' Her grandad finished the sentence. He grinned. He was sixty-five; a gardener, a walker, a cyclist. He was fit as a fiddle.

'Yes,' she admitted. 'Anyway, they're lovely clean animals, and you don't have to fuss them. They look after themselves, and—'

'Whoa!' her grandad said. 'Steady on!' He looked helplessly at his wife.

'Look, love,' her grandmother spoke gently. 'It's a good idea, and it's very good of you to be thinking of us like this, it really is. You're our beautiful, warm-hearted girl, you know that!'

Mandy saw a great big 'But' looming on the horizon. 'Yes?' she said, feeling her heart sink.

Her grandad took over. 'But we've just bought our smart new van. You know, our retirement treat!' He jerked his head sideways. 'There she stands in the drive all shiny and new, waiting to take us to the Italian Alps, to Provence, to Portugal!'

'To Scarborough, the day after tomorrow!' her grandmother put in.

Mandy nodded. 'So?'

'So we won't be at home to look after a pet as much as we were when your grandad was working. We'll be out on the open road, the autobahn, the freeway, with the wind in our hair and the sun on our faces!'

Mandy was shocked. She wondered if she'd ever see her grandparents again!

'Not all the time,' her grandad corrected. 'I still need to keep an eye on my tomatoes!'

'But too much of the time to be able to take in one of your stray kittens,' her grandmother said finally.

And Mandy had to accept that. Smoky was the one she'd been planning for them to have, with his cheeky face and his way of pushing the other three kittens out of the way when they were feeding. Now Smoky wouldn't be sunning himself on her grandad's patio after all. Mandy tried to swallow her disappointment.

'But …' her grandmother said, sweeping stray hair up into the pleat at the back of her head, 'we can still help!'

'How?' Mandy leapt at the promise. Her eyes lit up.

'We'll help you look for homes. How many kittens are there? Four?' Gran got on her thinking-cap. 'There's Eileen Davy at the Old School House, but she's on the main road, and she's already lost two cats to the traffic, poor things. There's Myra Hugill, but she has to look after her sick sister in York at present. There's Dora Janeki from Syke Farm, but she's a batty old thing and her new husband isn't known as an animal lover!'

Mandy seized each name, then let it drop as her grandmother counted them off on her fingers. She was beginning to feel hopeless again.

'Wait!' her grandad said. 'I've just had a brilliant idea!'

Mandy swung round to face him. 'What?'

'The post office!' he said, raising a finger.

Mandy looked puzzled. 'Not the post office just now, Grandad. We're talking about Walton's kittens!'

'I know. That's why I mentioned McFarlane's. That's my brilliant idea!'

'Oh, I see!' her grandmother said. 'Yes, Tom, of course!'

'What? What?' Mandy didn't see at all.

'The notice-board in the post office! That's what we need!' Her grandad took a postcard out of the bureau and uncapped his old fountain pen. 'Watch.'

He wrote in beautiful copperplate letters:

> WANTED!
> FOUR GOOD HOMES
> Cat lovers needed to provide homes for kittens.
> Please ring Welford 703267

'There!' he said, standing back and looking at his work of art. 'You can take it down to McFarlane's first thing in the morning!'

Mandy took the card. She nodded and smiled. 'Brilliant, Grandad!'

He screwed the top back on his pen. 'It's nothing, my dear,' he said modestly.

'Yes, it is, it's brilliant! We'll get millions of calls, you'll see!' Welford was full of animal lovers, and this was the perfect way to find them. Everyone went into the post office at some time during each day. Mandy hugged both her grandparents.

'Maybe not millions,' her grandmother advised.

'All right, dozens!' Mandy said, laughing at her own habit of exaggerating. They all laughed together.

She left the house, smiling and happy. She closed the gate with its Lilac Cottage sign, waved and set off down the lane. Tomorrow was Friday. She'd be down at McFarlane's with the lark, before the paper van or the milk delivery. She'd spend the weekend coping with all the phone calls. She ran home full of plans and preparations.

Mandy had arranged to meet James again to go into school early. She'd already been into the post office and pinned up her 'Wanted' card in pride of place on McFarlane's board. She greeted him cheerfully with, 'You're seven minutes late, James Hunter!'

James pushed his glasses back on to the bridge of his nose. 'Sorry,' he said. He screeched to a halt on his bike. 'I had to walk Blackie. Dad's away. And then I had to feed Benji.'

'Oh, well, then,' Mandy forgave him. Being late because of a dog and a cat was quite understandable. 'Let's go!'

They made up some time on the journey. Traffic was still light and they knew all the back ways. By five past eight they were knocking on the Williamses' kitchen door.

Mrs Williams opened it with a worried face. 'I thought you weren't coming! Come in, come in,' she said.

'Is something wrong?' Mandy was unpacking cat food and a carton of milk on to the kitchen table.

'I'm not sure. It's too quiet in there for my liking. Not like yesterday with all the racket. Even Eric noticed.' Mrs Williams watched anxiously.

Mandy lifted the basket lid. 'Hello, Walton!' she said. But the cat lay on her side and only managed a feeble miaow. 'Leave me in peace,' she seemed to say. She raised her head, but she didn't stretch and make her way out into the daylight to sort out some breakfast.

'Poor thing, she's exhausted!' Mandy said. 'James, you'd better open that can of food. I'll fetch her out.' She reached in, tenderly lifting out the tired cat. 'She'll be all right in a bit,' she told Mrs Williams. She knew from helping out at home that there was nothing seriously wrong. 'She just needs looking after.' And she set her down to feed.

Walton wobbled, steadied and settled eagerly to the dish of meat.

'What about the kittens?' James said.

Mandy cast an expert eye over the four huddled shapes. 'Fine!' she said. 'But we'll have to feed them. We'll need the droppers. And we'll have to use the ordinary carton milk for now.' She'd seen her mum and dad do it often enough. Now she hoped she could manage it all by herself.

James fetched the droppers from her bag. Mandy gently heated the milk. Then she lifted one of the feather-light bundles. She sat with it on her lap and eased open its tiny mouth. 'Come on, Patch, come on!' she coaxed.

She squeezed the rubber bulb of the dropper and took in milk from the warm pan. Then, while she held open the kitten's mouth with two fingers, she eased the glass tube between its lips with the other hand. She squeezed again and watched Patch's tiny tongue lick and then swallow the liquid. 'See?' she said to James. 'Now you have a go.'

He nodded and took another kitten, Smoky, out of the basket. Afraid but determined, he copied Mandy's actions with a second dropper. Smoky looked surprised, then gulped. James looked up in triumph.

'Well done!' Mandy said.

It was fifteen minutes later and they were just finishing with the last two kittens when Mr Williams tramped back in from unlocking the school. James and Mandy were busy stroking the kittens' throats to encourage them to swallow. Mr Williams heard the tiny mewing from the basket. 'What's up with the mother cat then?' he barked.

'Tired out,' Mrs Williams said. 'And you would be too.' She hovered by the sink like a worried relative.

'Hmm.' He turned back out of his kitchen, grumbling.

'This place is being turned into a cat hospital! A man can't even call his home his own any more!'

Mandy and James finished the feeding and cleared up the room to perfection. Walton was sitting on the step, taking the morning sun. She gave herself a thorough licking. Mandy bent to stroke her. 'Good girl,' she said. She was relieved when Walton decided it was time to return to her kittens. They watched her walk across the shiny tiles, jump up and nimbly lift the basket lid with one paw. Then she disappeared from sight.

'Clever thing!' James said. He looked at his watch. 'It's a quarter to nine,' he reminded Mandy.

They said a hurried goodbye to Mrs Williams and ran out through the garden and across the playground. A strong wind blew white blossom petals diagonally across the tarmac. 'What do you think?' James asked, pausing before they passed under the great stone arch of the main entrance.

'Oh, Walton will be all right,' Mandy said. 'She'll just have to take things easy.' She hitched her schoolbag higher on to her shoulder and brushed cat hairs off her navy blue skirt. 'But I'm not so sure about the kittens now.'

Mandy didn't want to scare James, but she thought the cat's milk might dry up. This sometimes happened when the mother wasn't strong. If so, the tiny things would soon starve to death. 'We'll have to wait and see.

Perhaps Walton will be able to go on feeding them herself.'

'What if she can't?' James wanted to know.

Mandy thought of the kittens with their gradually opening eyes, their fluffier coats, their attempts to struggle up on to all fours. They still tumbled and collapsed like rag-dolls. She could hold them easily in the palm of her hand. 'Well, we'll just have to carry on feeding them ourselves,' she said.

All morning long Mandy had kitten worries on her mind. There was the old one of finding four good homes in less than a week, and the new one which she wouldn't confess even to James. But the question kept crowding in on her. It wouldn't go away. Walton was exhausted from the birth. The kittens were clinging on to life by a thread. And the question still whirled in her head as Mandy sat and ate her packed lunch in B Hall with Kate and Melanie: would they need to find homes for the kittens after all? Would the poor little things even survive?

Four

Mandy decided that the best answer to her question was a great big 'yes'!

You have to think 'yes' all the time, or life will get you down, she told herself. She and James would hand-rear the kittens if necessary. So she set about finding homes for them with even more energy than before.

She and James fed Walton and the little gang of kittens straight after school, then they cycled back to Animal Ark. 'We're going to make more notices!' Mandy announced. She led James upstairs and scrabbled under her bed, looking for some luminous pink card she'd stored there before Christmas. 'Then we'll be sure that every single person in Welford will read one!'

She liked to work in her room; it was an art gallery of animal posters. Horses and rabbits, dogs and cats stared down from her walls. Hardly a centimetre of wallpaper showed through, just how Mandy liked it. Mandy and James knelt on the floor to cut small rectangles of pink card. They chose broad black felt-tips and began designing their own ads. 'Where will we stick these?' James wanted to know.

'Shh, I'm thinking!' Mandy said. She wanted eyecatching words to draw people's attention. Finally she wrote in big capital letters:

KITTENS IN THE KITCHEN
Bring love into your life.
Cats make cosy companions.
Adopt a kitten. Ring Welford 703267.

It was catchier than her grandad's notice. She was pleased as she knelt back to judge the effect, while James finished his much more practical card:

HOMES NEEDED FOR FOUR KITTENS!
Remember, pets are for life!
If interested, ring Welford 703267

'I could put this one on your board in reception,' he suggested.

Mandy nodded. 'Good idea. Let's go down and ask Jean before she finishes for the day.' She knew Jean liked to know exactly what went up on the notice-board in reception.

They went downstairs and through into Animal Ark. Jean had closed the appointment book and was searching for her car keys. She had been their receptionist for five years and she was always losing her keys. Mandy knew all the places they were likely to be. She set about helping Jean search.

'Here they are!' Mandy lifted the blue book and handed the keys to Jean.

'Oh, silly me!' Jean said, as she always did. She wore her glasses on a silver chain round her neck and still managed to forget where she'd put them.

James tried not to smile. 'Can we put a "Homes Wanted" notice on your board, please?' he said.

Jean took the card, looked for her glasses, found them hanging down her chest and read the words. 'That looks fine. Just find a space over there beside all the others,' she said.

'Others?' James looked at Mandy. They scrambled across to the board. In the bottom corner there were at least six other 'Homes Wanted' cards. James and Mandy's faces fell a little.

'Only three of them are for kittens,' James said. Two others were for puppies, one for a pony.

Mandy counted up quickly. 'Yes, but that's fourteen kittens needing homes altogether!' Fourteen kittens in a tiny place the size of Welford.

'Come on, chop-chop!' Jean said. She was busy locking cupboards, windows, drawers and anything else that stood still. 'I want to shut up shop!'

They looked again at the notices, trying not to feel downhearted. 'Ours is the brightest card!' James said. 'And it's in the best position!'

Mandy agreed. 'I've had another idea!'

With the second bright pink card in her hand

they shot off ahead of Jean, up the drive and down into the village. 'It's Friday. Gran will be playing badminton!' They cycled on past the post office, towards the village hall.

'So?' James overtook Mandy. His football training was coming in handy for stamina. They made for the hall, which was set back from the road, next to the church.

'They've got a Women's Institute notice-board in the entrance,' Mandy reminded him.

'Right.' James nodded and kept up the pace. Lots of kind-hearted ladies came to the village hall to do flower arranging and cake icing, besides the Friday evening badminton club. It was a great position for one of their cards.

They almost bumped into Miss Davy from the Old School House as she came out of the hall, racquet in hand and not a silver-blue hair out of place. She turned and called in a shrill voice, 'Dorothy, one granddaughter!' She smiled at them and continued on her way.

Gran emerged, red-faced and breathless. She wore a bright turquoise tracksuit. 'Mandy!' She gave her a quick peck on the cheek. 'How nice. But it's thirteen-eleven, final game. I can only spare a second!'

'Sorry, Gran.' Mandy held up her KITTENS IN THE KITCHEN card. 'Can we pin this on the notice-board?'

Mrs Hope squinted at it. 'Oh, the kittens? Yes, yes, of course. Good idea. 'Bye, love!' And she dashed back to finish her game.

Mandy opened the glass door of the notice-board and made space between lists of flower rotas for the church, Brownie parades and a whist drive. She pinned her notice firmly in the centre, closed the door, stood back and admired it.

'Better!' James said.

They were pleased with the evening's work as they finally said goodbye and headed home.

After supper Mr Hope took Mandy into Animal Ark with a secret smile on his face. 'Come and see a new admission,' he invited.

Near the door of the residential unit was one of the see-through cages, shaped like a cat basket but made of clear plastic. Mr Hope picked it up.

'What is it?' Mandy could see the usual newspaper nest and a roll of soft grey rag, but she couldn't spot any animal in there.

'Squirrel!' Mr Hope said. A small black nose peeped out of the newspapers. 'A baby. Five weeks old.' Two large black eyes appeared, and out it came, the size of a hamster, with a long, long tail. Mr Hope unlatched the cage door and lifted it out. He handed the little grey squirrel to Mandy.

'Oh!' she said. She was speechless with delight. She felt its sharp little feet. She stroked its soft grey back while the baby tried to suck the end of her finger. 'Where's its mother?' she asked.

'She got run over.'

Mandy gasped, and her face crumpled.

'Yes, I know,' he said, looking at her. 'And this little one would have died if someone hadn't found him.'

Mandy shook her head. Life could be so cruel.

'You'll never guess who brought him in.'

'Who?'

'Old Ernie Bell from the cottages behind the Fox and Goose.'

Mandy looked surprised. She knew Ernie Bell as a grumpy, silent old man who shuffled down the village street with his bag of shopping.

'He came in and handed him over. "'Ere, veterinary," he says to poor Jean, "just check 'im over while I fix up a run for 'im in my backyard. I'll be back for 'im in twenty-four hours. Just check 'e's all right!" And he leaves the little chap with Jean and stomps off to build a wire netting run. Who'd have believed it?' Ernie didn't have the reputation of being soft on animals. Mr Hope put the baby back in its cage.

'What's the roll of cloth for, Dad?' Mandy bent down to study the squirrel in his cage.

'For comfort; something for him to snuggle up to. Animals need a mother substitute, you know. Something to take the dead mother's place.' His voice was warm. He put an arm round Mandy.

'What are you feeding him with?'

'This stuff. It's the bottle food we give to orphan kittens. Why?'

Mandy was making new plans for Walton's brood. She took the box of white powder and read the list of contents and instructions printed on the side. 'Can I buy some of this from this week's pocket money?' she asked.

'For your school kittens?' Mr Hope lifted

three boxes down from the shelf. 'Go on, take them. You don't have to pay!'

Mandy smiled. 'Walton's a bit weak at the moment. We'll have to help her feed the kittens properly.'

'Well, this stuff is much better than cows' milk,' Mr Hope said, adding an extra box. 'Mix it with boiled water, and use these little bottles with rubber teats. The kittens can suck these properly. Everything's sterilised of course.'

'How often?' Mandy realised that there was a proper way to do this. The kittens' lives depended on it.

'Every couple of hours for the first week.'

Mandy gulped.

'Less if the mother cat can still give milk herself, during the night for instance.'

'I think she can. She's just a very small cat and she's tired.' Mandy was still determined to think the best.

'Well, then, this stuff four times a day will do the trick. Breakfast, lunch, tea, supper.' He glanced at Mandy's serious face. 'You're going to be busy,' he said. 'Any luck with finding homes for them yet?'

'Not yet.' She bent thoughtfully to the level

of the baby squirrel in the cage. 'Will Mr Bell have to let him go eventually, back into the wild?'

Her dad shook his head. 'He's not allowed to. It's against the law, I'm afraid. That's because he'd never survive out in the wild now. Poor little chap, it seems he'll have to make do with Ernie's backyard for the rest of his life!'

Mandy nodded.

'Don't worry, there are worse fates,' Mr Hope said.

'Oh, I know.' But Mandy was still in a serious mood as she cycled over to school with the special kitten food. True, like Ernie Bell and the little squirrel, she was giving the kittens a chance of life. But without homes, would it be a life worth living?

She cycled and prayed that the notices in the post office, Animal Ark and the village hall would work. She wondered too whether she could persuade Mr Williams to give them a bit more time. A week was so short! She leaned her bike against the hedge and went up the steps into the caretaker's kitchen.

Once Walton was happily feeding, Mandy

showed Mrs Williams the new arrangements for Smoky, Patch, Amy and Eric. To her surprise, the caretaker's wife actually offered to help. 'Don't tell my husband!' She pressed her thin lips tightly together. 'He wouldn't approve!' She took Amy out of the basket and gingerly snuggled her up against her flowered apron, complete with feeding bottle. 'Poor little scrap!' she murmured.

Mandy smiled. 'She's fine. Look, she's hungry!'

Mrs Williams sat happily while the kitten fed. 'You mustn't mind my Eric,' she confided. 'I know he must seem like a grumpy old nuisance to you, but he's not so bad really.'

'No.' Mandy tried to believe it. All she could think of were Mr Williams's big boots and his loud voice. Hands as big as shovels. Temper like a volcano.

'You must think he's a stubborn old mule.'

'No!' Mandy knew she didn't sound sincere.

'Yes!' Mrs Williams looked down into the kitten's face. 'Yes, you do. But he loves his garden!' She bent sideways towards Mandy. 'Do you know, he keeps a squeezy bottle full of water out there on the porch. If a cat comes anywhere near his roses looking as if it's going to dig, Eric's out with the bottle, shooting at it. You should hear him when he scores a direct hit!'

'One wet cat!' Mandy joined in the laughter. 'I was thinking he might give us a bit longer than a week,' she said. 'Even when we find homes for them, Walton will have to go on looking after them for quite a bit. The less we need to move them around the better.' She looked pleadingly at Mrs Williams. 'Maybe you could persuade him?'

'Hope by name, hopeful by nature!' Mrs Williams said. But she was shaking her head. 'No, I know Eric. He's made up his mind!'

'Can't you just try?' Mandy was busy tidying up bottles and saucers.

But this time Mrs Williams wouldn't bend. 'No, it's not fair to him. He won't come into his own kitchen as it is. I know, I know,' she interrupted Mandy's protest, 'it's not sensible. But Eric's not always a sensible man. Who is? I'll tell you something else. He has a lot of pain, bending and kneeling and suchlike. Arthritis. In the knees. Very painful.' She lowered her voice. 'To tell you the truth we don't mention it in case the school gets to hear. He's worried about his job!'

Mandy nodded. Suddenly Mr Williams seemed human after all. 'I'm sorry to hear that.'

'Well, don't say I told you,' Mrs Williams warned. They were standing out on the porch. Walton was perched on the rim of the laundry basket licking herself clean. 'He's out at his darts match this evening. It cheers him up.'

Mrs Williams stared up at the pebbled clouds. 'But Eric's a worried man. It's the job, the house, everything. And the pain, of course. I can't even get him to go to a doctor.' She glanced at Mandy. 'So, you see, I can't ask him to do any more, can I? He's done enough already.'

Mandy agreed and smiled sadly. She rode home slowly. She understood more about Mr Williams's bad temper now, that was certain. But it didn't stop time passing. The sand was running steadily through the hour-glass. They had five days left!

Five

'Hello, Welford 703267?' a woman's voice asked.

'This is it!' Mandy yelped, then lowered her voice to speak into the phone. 'Yes, this is Welford 703267.' She held her breath. 'Who's speaking please?' She gave her mother a hopeful thumbs up sign.

'Hello?' The voice sounded shy and cautious. There was a long pause.

'Hello, this is Amanda Hope. Who's speaking, please?' Mandy made a face of pretend panic at her mum.

'Hello, I want Welford 703267.' The voice

seemed strange, and unused to the telephone.

'Can I help you, please?' Mandy said firmly. What was going on here? Her mum had paused over the washing-up and was trying to listen in.

'Did you put a notice in the post office?' the woman on the end of the phone asked. 'Are you the person with the kittens?'

'I am!' Mandy said with a grin. 'I take it you're looking for a kitten?' Mrs Hope winked and carried on with the breakfast things.

There was a long, crackly pause. 'My name is Miss Marjorie Spry. I live at The Riddings. Please come to see me at two o'clock precisely.'

Then the phone went dead.

'Well?' Mrs Hope said.

Relief swept over her as Mandy realised that their plan was beginning to work. It was only nine o'clock on Saturday morning, and they'd already got a response! 'Yes!' she yelled, nearly jumping for joy. 'I'm off to tell Grandad!'

'Mandy, what if there are any more phone calls?' Mrs Hope was drying her hands, following her out.

'Write down the numbers on that pad, will

you, Mum? I'm so thrilled I can hardly wait!' She rushed up the lane without a jacket. It was drizzling but she didn't care.

Her grandparents were stacking tins of soup inside the tiny cupboard aboard their camper. 'Tomato, minestrone, cream of chicken!' Her gran handed them up to her grandad and ticked them off her list.

'Tin-opener?' Her grandfather popped his head out of the sliding door. He saw Mandy. 'Hello, love!'

'It's worked! It's worked!' she greeted them. 'Your brilliant card, Grandad, it's worked!'

He rubbed his hands. Mandy's grandparents both stood there in their twin Aran sweaters, the drizzle wetting their grey hair. 'Has it now? You've got a response then?'

'Of course she's got a response, haven't you, Mandy?' Gran put in. 'Come inside. We're all getting wet.'

'Who is it then?' her grandad asked as he put on the kettle. 'Anyone we know?'

'It's someone called Spy. No, Spry. That's it, Miss Marjorie Spry!'

Gran shut the kitchen door firmly and wiped her feet. Her head went on to one side. 'The Riddings, isn't it?'

'Yes, The Riddings. Why, what's the matter? Do you know her?'

Her grandmother straightened herself up and bustled with the cups and saucers. 'Yes. She lives at the big house out on the Walton Road. Set back from the road. You know, the big old house!'

'I know!' Mandy said. They passed it every day on the way to school. It was well away from the traffic, with a huge lawned garden. The perfect place for a cat to live! 'She wants me to go and see her there at two o'clock this afternoon.'

'Does she now?' her grandmother said. 'That'll be one for the record book!'

'Why? What do you mean?' Mandy was nearly bursting with impatience. 'I thought you'd be pleased!'

'We are, love,' her grandad soothed.

'They're not usually keen on visitors, that's all,' Gran explained. 'In fact, I believe the last person they had over their threshold was Mr Lovejoy, the old vicar before Mr Walters, and that must be over five years ago!'

'No!' Mandy couldn't believe it.

'Yes, when their father died the two sisters went into a sort of hibernation. It's true!' Gran insisted. 'Still, that won't make any difference to you, I don't expect. If Miss Marjorie Spry wants to see you about a kitten and she's asked you along, you go and see her.' She patted Mandy's hand. 'They're harmless. A bit peculiar, but harmless enough.'

'Anyway, it's best to check these places before you send these precious kittens off to their new homes,' her grandad agreed. 'You've got to see if they're the right sort of thing!'

Mandy nodded, but she refused to be put off her stride.

'Take someone along with you,' her grandad suggested. 'Just to be on the safe side.'

'James will come with me,' Mandy said. She lifted a cardboard box full of bread, cornflakes, milk and margarine. 'Where do you want me to put these?'

Together they finished packing for 'the great trial run', as her grandad called it. He meant their first expedition in their new camper. Finally they were ready.

'Map?' Grandad said, climbing into the driving seat.

'Map!' Gran produced it from the passenger shelf.

He turned on the windscreen wipers. 'Wellington boots? Storm capes? Sou'westers?'

Gran flipped the map at him. 'Ready?' she laughed. They waved to Mandy. 'To sunny Scarborough!' she cried.

Mandy watched them disappear into the drizzle. There were still four hours to go before the visit to The Riddings. She would ring James to arrange to meet him, then fill up the morning with little jobs at Animal Ark, and of course by cycling over to feed Walton and the kittens.

Two o'clock came at last. They arrived to find the front lawn of The Riddings spread out like a cricket pitch. James and Mandy decided to leave their bikes at the gate.

'I wonder who cuts this grass?' James said. It went in neat strips, light and dark. The edges were neatly clipped.

'I do!' An ancient man in corduroy trousers growled at them from behind a laurel hedge. He was bent almost double, probably from years and years of clipping the edges of huge lawns,

Mandy guessed. 'Have you come about a kitten?' he growled again.

They nodded.

'Miss Marjorie warned me about it. "Geoffrey," she said, "show the girl up to the door!" So I'm following orders. This way!' He trudged ahead of them up the gravel drive.

The house was as big as a hotel, built of stone, with pointed towers at each corner and battlements along the roof. It was covered in ivy. Though they passed it every day, James and Mandy could truly say that they'd never really paid much attention to it before. It had arched windows, stone pillars and massive steps up to a wide front door. 'Like a setting for a horror film!' Mandy whispered nervously.

Just when they felt they needed him most, their guide left them. 'This is as far as I ever go. Ring three times,' he said. 'Nice and loud, mind. You might have to wait.' And he went off, bowed and grumbling, to shave the lawn.

They looked at each other, shrugged, then James rang the bell. Silence. He rang again. And again. Finally someone began rattling locks on the other side of the massive door. 'Wait!' a tiny voice ordered.

'What do you think we're doing?' James whispered to Mandy, trying not to laugh.

'Shh!' Mandy said. They had to be on their best behaviour.

But even Mandy couldn't stop her jaw from hanging wide when the door finally creaked open.

The hall was the size of a ballroom, all in pink marble, with dark wood panels and glass chandeliers. But it was dull with age, and grey with years of neglect. What had once been as splendid as a fairytale had now decayed.

'Yes?' A lady stood before them. Her stick-like arms and legs poked out from a moth-eaten cream silk dressing-gown. She peered at them like a bat in the light.

'Miss Spry?' Mandy said uncertainly. A loud voice would have knocked the old lady down flat, she was sure.

'Yes!' She blinked her watery grey eyes. A skinny hand clutched the neck of her dressing-gown. 'We don't see visitors!' she chattered.

Mandy's grandmother had been right. No one had stepped this way for years. Curtains were closed to keep out the daylight. A collection of old blue and white china

ornaments cluttered the window-sills. Great piles of yellow newspapers were heaped on shelves. 'Miss Marjorie Spry?' Mandy repeated, her heart sinking as her eyes took in the mess.

'Joan! Joan!' the woman shrieked. She began to close the door in their faces, but it was big and heavy. They saw the figure of another thin little woman come hurrying downstairs.

'Come in, come in,' this second person ordered in a thin voice. She was beckoning to them, half running across the hall. 'They've come about the kitten, Joan. Now open the door at once!'

And there they stood, two ladies thin as sticks, wild-haired, in matching silk robes. They had the same sharp faces. They had movements which mirrored each other, and voices which echoed and mocked. Identical twins! Miss Joan and Miss Marjorie Spry!

'We don't want visitors!' the first one, Miss Joan, repeated with a birdlike twitch of her head.

'Yes, we do. I invited them!' Miss Marjorie argued. 'I want a kitten for this dreadful old place. I want to bring some life in here!'

Miss Joan stared stubbornly, silently back at her sister. Her hand stayed poised to slam the door shut.

'I do, Joan! I'm tired of living in this old museum of a place. I want some life. We're not old yet; let's make a fresh start!' Miss Marjorie pleaded. 'Look, this girl is advertising kittens. So let her in!'

At last Miss Joan gave way. Fascinated, Mandy and James stepped inside. To them it seemed like actually stepping into the past, into a kind of prison. Miss Joan pushed the door closed after them. It shut with a dull, heavy click. 'What kittens?' Miss Joan challenged. She looked her sister in the face. 'Who told me anything about a kitten?'

'I told you!' Miss Marjorie snapped. 'An advert in the post office. Welford 703627!'

'But I don't like kittens!' Miss Joan protested. 'You know that!'

Mandy stood in the middle of their argument, her heart sinking right into her shoes by now. Miss Joan would never give in over this. Anyway, who'd want to leave a kitten where it wasn't wanted one hundred per cent by everyone in the house? She looked at James and could tell that he thought the same. They both sighed.

They watched as Miss Marjorie grew more and more angry. 'How do you know you don't like kittens?' Her eyes seemed to spark. 'Have you had one? Have you ever owned a cat in your entire life? Have you? Have you?'

She turned to face Mandy and James, smouldering with rage. '*I* like cats! Joan likes cats, though she says she doesn't! She only says it to be awkward. Yes you do!' she snapped at her twin. 'She's just a spoilsport. It's because it's *my* idea to bring a kitten to The Riddings, to help bring the place back to life a bit. She says no to all my ideas!' She nearly cried with exasperation. The tiny twins stood face to face like featherweight boxers.

'Anyway, I'm the older twin!' Miss Marjorie said grandly. 'And I have decided. Don't listen to her!'

'Well, they're still very young at present,' Mandy began to explain. 'We're only trying to sort out suitable homes for them in the future, you see.' Still she couldn't settle those doubts about this being a good place to bring one of her precious kittens.

'Where is it?' The older twin began poking at

Mandy and James as if Amy might be hidden in one of their pockets.

'She's still with her mother. We're just starting to look, as I said.'

'Not here? Not brought it with you?' Miss Marjorie said sharply.

'Ha, ha, ha!' Miss Joan sang out. She did a little dance of delight. 'Ha, ha, ha!'

Miss Marjorie's thin patience finally snapped. 'Quiet!' she bellowed. She picked up an old black umbrella from the stand and launched it like a javelin at her noisy sister. It missed by miles, but Miss Joan froze on the spot. Then she grabbed a newspaper from a shelf and rolled it up like a baseball bat. James and Mandy stood with their mouths open. Who would believe them?

'Joan!' Miss Marjorie warned.

'You threw something at me first!' Miss Joan retaliated.

'Get out!' Miss Marjorie cried. 'Get out, get out!'

James and Mandy didn't know if she meant them or her sister. Everything was chaos. Mandy was growing sure of just one thing, though: this was no place for tiny Amy.

She knew this once and for all when Miss Joan, in her mischief, raised her rolled newspaper and began to chase Miss Marjorie from the hall into the study, a room at the front of the house. In a panic to stop them injuring each other, Mandy and James scuttled after.

Mandy stopped short. The room was lined from ceiling to floor with old books. But on the many tables scattered about the room were glass cases, dozens of them. Inside the dusty cases, perched, poised and perfectly preserved, were . . . stuffed animals!

A heron stood on one leg, forever fishing. An otter bared his teeth at an invisible enemy. A wildcat stared warily out, as if he knew he was about to be made extinct in Britain. Mandy squealed. Both hands flew to her cheeks.

'Let's go!' James said. For once, he took the lead. He grabbed her hand and made a run for it, back through the littered hall. They didn't turn to see if they were being followed. They just ran.

'Hey, you two!' Miss Marjorie called.

But they covered the distance to the gate in record time, ignoring the grinning gardener as they fled. Outside the gate they paused for breath. 'Well?' James gasped.

'No good,' Mandy said, almost in tears. The door was closed, the ivy still smothered the walls. The house seemed empty and grim. It would be another five years before anyone dared to disturb it.

'I agree.' They were both too shocked to think straight.

It was only the routine of cycling over to look after things in the Williamses' kitchen that saved them. They fed the kittens and cycled home to news from Mandy's mum.

Mrs Hope smiled across the treatment table where she was giving Snap the terrier his final injection. 'A Mrs Parker Smythe has been on the phone,' she said. 'She says she's interested in one of the kittens!'

Six

Mandy was up in good time next day. She'd done her chores, been over to feed Walton, and was back before her mum had finished breakfast.

'I'll take you up to the Parker Smythes in the car, if you like,' Mrs Hope offered. 'The arrangement was for nine-thirty.' It was the only other phone call about the kittens since the Misses Spry disaster, so Mandy felt glad her mother was coming along to give moral support.

'It's way out of the village, up by the Beacon.' Mrs Hope opened the passenger door of their big four-wheel drive. 'Hop in,' she said. 'Do we have to call for James as well?'

'No. He came over earlier to feed the kittens, but he's got a football match today, and his mum told him to take Blackie on an extra long walk, so he can't come.'

'Do the Hunters still have that cat of theirs?' Mrs Hope fastened her seat belt.

'Benji? Yes, course. Why?'

'He's getting on a bit, that's all.'

They took the high road out of Welford. Soon a steep hill loomed ahead of them. On top there was a stone pillar, visible for miles around: the Beacon.

'I expect James is still recovering from yesterday?' Mrs Hope said, her eyes set firmly on the road ahead. She went rapidly down the gears.

Mandy nodded. 'We both are.' Mandy was brave, but even she was rattled by the Spry sisters. She reckoned she was the least squeamish person around; she'd watched operations on stomachs, intestines, legs and hearts. But she shuddered at the memory of the poor stuffed creatures in the library at The Riddings; glass-eyed, covered in dust.

'You have to remember it was the fashion a hundred years ago. Most people have thrown those glass cases full of birds and animals away by now. But don't blame the twins too much. Poor things.' Mrs Hope spoke quietly. She pushed a stray strand of hair behind her ear.

'Yes,' Mandy agreed. 'Animals look so much better alive and out in the wild, not stuffed inside some rotten case!'

'I meant the sisters!' Her mum glanced across at her. The hill was beginning to flatten out now. They could see the Beacon just ahead. 'They don't mean anyone any harm.'

'What, those two horrible old things! Nobody ever goes near them and all they ever do is argue!'

'Exactly,' Mrs Hope said softly.

And Mandy had to sit and think about that one as they pulled up outside a high hawthorn hedge with double iron gates, electronically controlled. 'Beacon House' was written in big gold letters. And 'No Parking. Trespassers will be prosecuted.'

Mrs Hope put on the handbrake. 'Anyway, this looks more straightforward.' She spoke into a little security machine on the gatepost, then the gate opened, as if by magic.

Mandy turned and took in the long distance view of the valley; its odd-shaped patchwork fields, scattered hillside farms, the road and river running parallel along the bottom, and Welford's two main streets criss-crossing in the far distance.

Then she turned again and followed her mother up the drive. They went on foot through a small bluebell wood, up to the big white house.

'What's that?' Mandy whispered. She pointed to a flat tarmac area the size of a tennis court, but marked with large white circles. It wasn't a tennis court anyway, because that was on the other side, to the right of the house.

'Helicopter pad?' Mrs Hope suggested. She rang the doorbell.

Mandy gulped. A very blonde, very smart woman opened the door. She was dressed in white shirt and trousers, with gold necklaces, rings, bracelets. A lot of gold. Even her shoes had gold decorations sewn on.

Mandy felt her mother give her a little shove forward to speak. 'Mrs Parker Smythe?' she asked nervously.

The woman nodded. Her blonde hair stayed put. Not a highlighted strand moved. Her smile revealed two rows of perfectly even, perfectly white teeth between shiny pink lips. 'Come in!' she said, like you heard it said in posh films, usually with 'darling' on the end.

They went in and she closed the door. 'Come this way!' she said, all teeth and lipstick, and gold bits dangling. Through the white hall with Italian tiles and rugs, into the kitchen. 'You must be Mandy? You put the nice pink advert in the village hall? I was collecting Imogen from the Brownies and we saw your notice!' she gushed.

Mandy nodded. She was finding it hard to fit in a word. Anyway, the kitchen made her feel that being there in her jeans and T-shirt and talking out loud in her ordinary voice was a bit of a mistake. It wasn't a bit like the old pine table and quarry-tiled floor of her own kitchen. This had shiny blue glass bowls and white gadgets everywhere, and no food anywhere to be seen.

Mrs Parker Smythe didn't seem to notice Mandy's shyness. 'Imogen is my little girl. She's seven!' she said proudly, as if Imogen being seven was like winning the Olympic Games single-handed.

'And this is Ronald, my husband. He's in satellite television!'

A balding man walked in, nodded and walked out again. He wore the palest yellow V-necked sweater and fawn checked trousers.

'He's going to play golf,' Mrs Parker Smythe told them. She shared another confidence: 'With Jason Shaw! You know, Jason Shaw, the actor! They're very good friends, Ronald and Jason!'

Mandy risked a glance at her mother, but didn't dare ask, 'Jason who?' Her mother was looking steadily out of the window, trying not to smile.

'We first met Jason when he came to film here, you know,' Mrs Parker Smythe rattled on. 'For an episode of *The Swallows in Spring*, this time last year. They used our swimming-pool!'

Mandy gulped again. She couldn't help it. Maybe tough little Smoky would be the right kitten for the Parker Smythes. The rough and tumble one. He'd bring them down to earth.

'Yes, our swimming-pool was used as a set for the programme. It belongs to the right period for the series. So Jason and the crew came up. That's how we met!' Mrs Parker Smythe bubbled on. She seemed to have forgotten all about the reason for their visit.

'Did you want a kitten for your little girl?' Mandy managed to fit in at last. Mr Parker Smythe wandered in and out again, apparently looking for something.

'Yes, well we have so much space here.' Mrs Parker Smythe spread her arms and her jewellery jangled. 'And such a big garden! And of course we have security cameras out there, so there's no danger of the poor little mite getting lost or anything!'

Mandy noticed her mother's eyebrows shoot up a fraction of a centimetre.

'And when we're away at our house in Tuscany, we still have Mrs Bates, our housekeeper, to come in and look after the kitten, feed it and so on.' Mrs Parker Smythe looked at her gold watch. 'Would you please excuse me a moment?' She dashed off after her husband.

'I wonder what he's lost,' Mandy whispered.

'His helicopter?' her mum said. But no; they heard huge blades begin to whir out on the pad. Clearly it had been wheeled out from its hangar and prepared for take-off.

They grinned. Mandy felt more relaxed. 'What if Smoky doesn't fit in here because he's only a plain, ordinary moggie?'

'Let's meet the little girl first, before we make any decisions,' Mrs Hope said.

Mandy nodded. She had to admit, once again, the signs were not all that promising.

'Oh, good, you're still here!' Mrs Parker Smythe floated back in after a few minutes. 'Now you must come through. Come and meet Imogen!'

She led them out of the kitchen across a giant conservatory full of artificial palms and pink-flowered cane furniture. But this was only a link to the house's main attraction; its indoor heated pool. This opened up from the conservatory through wide double doors.

The poolside was dazzling white and the water was deep blue. There was a fountain at one end, and windows from ceiling to floor all down one side. And there in the water, swimming like a walrus with just its nose and whiskers out of the water, was Imogen Parker Smythe.

'Imogen!' her mother called, clapping her jewelled hands smartly.

Imogen ignored her.

'Imogen, we have visitors!' her mother called again.

No response. Imogen swam round and round the fountain at the deep end. Mandy was amazed by her rudeness. *I'd never get away with that!* she thought.

Mrs Parker Smythe sighed. 'Come along, we'd better go down.' She went along the poolside carrying an apricot coloured bathrobe and a towel for her daughter. Mandy and Mrs Hope followed.

'Imogen!' Mrs Parker Smythe said in a coaxing voice. She crouched beside the water. 'Now come along, darling. Come and talk to Mummy about a sweetie, itsy bitsy little kittie for Immikins!'

Mandy swallowed hard. She stuck both hands into her jeans pockets. *Yuk!* she thought. She just hoped no one could read her mind.

'Shan't!' Imogen retorted, swimming in smaller circles.

'Oh, come on, darling! Remember, we talked about a sweet little furry kittie for you just this morning at breakfast. Remember?'

'No!' Imogen spat out water like a whale.

'Immie!' Mrs Parker Smythe was getting wet. 'Now come along out of there immediately, or I'll call your daddy!'

With a great sigh and much splashing Imogen Parker Smythe heaved herself out of the water. She was a mousy-haired, slightly overweight little girl with a constant scowl. She squirmed as her mother wrapped her in the bathrobe. She pushed away the towel offered for her dripping hair. Instead, she shook her head from side to side like a dog.

'Hello,' Mandy said. She forced herself to take the lead in this conversation.

Imogen tossed her head and sniffed up great drips of water.

'I hear you want a kitten?' Mandy went on.

Sniff. Sniff.

'I've got four kittens. Four tiny ones just a few days old. But soon their mother will finish feeding them, and after that they'll need really good names and somebody to look after them!' Mandy explained in what she thought was a clear, sensible way.

'I know that!' Imogen snorted. 'Everyone knows that!'

'Immie!' Mrs Parker Smythe chirped.

'They'll need good homes, and someone very kind and careful to look after them!' Mandy said in a much cooler voice.

'What colour are they?' Imogen demanded, eye to eye with Mandy. 'I want a white one!'

Mandy paused. 'Well, the colour isn't that important really, is it? I mean, a kitten isn't a kind of toy, is it? It's a real live animal, you know. Soon it'll grow into a big cat that will still need feeding and taking to the vet, and somewhere clean and airy to sleep. In fact, it will need lots of looking after!'

Imogen turned to her mother. 'I only want a white one!' she whined.

'But, Immikins!' Mrs Parker Smythe looked helplessly at Mandy.

'You said I could have a white one!' The child stamped her foot. 'A white kitten! A fluffy white one with long fur! I want one! I want one!'

Mandy was furious. She felt like stepping right up to the revolting girl and pushing her back into the swimming-pool. 'Kittens are not toys!' she repeated. 'And they don't have to match your colour scheme!'

'Mandy!' Mrs Hope warned under her breath.

But Imogen was equal to the fight. She took a long look at Mandy, then she screwed her face tight and whined loudly. 'O-o-oh, Mummy, make the horrible nasty girl go away! I don't like her! Make her go away, Mummy!'

Mrs Parker Smythe fell for it. 'There, there, Immikins, don't cry!' she said. She cuddled her daughter at a distance, so as to keep dry. 'You don't have to have a kittie if you don't want one, darling. There, there!'

Mandy saw Imogen's face peep out at her from behind podgy little fists. Imogen sneered up at her. 'That got you!' she seemed to be saying.

Mrs Hope was pulling at Mandy's arm. 'Time to go,' she urged.

But Mrs Parker Smythe had left off cuddling Imogen and came towards them. 'Take no notice,' she whispered. 'Imogen's in one of her moods. You can bring the kitten anyway. I'll talk her round.'

But Mandy stood her ground. She was determined to have her say. 'Mrs Parker Smythe,' she announced, 'I'm afraid this would never work!'

Mrs Parker Smythe's gold jewellery trembled

as she went back and bent over her daughter.

Mandy continued. 'To keep a pet you have to be a sensible, caring person. Animals have rights, you know, and one of those rights is to belong to a good, responsible owner!' She paused for breath, but there was no stopping her now. 'And I'm afraid Imogen just doesn't qualify! I couldn't imagine anyone *less* suited to look after Smoky, Patch, Amy or Eric!'

She glared down at them as they hugged each other by the side of their swanky pool. She turned on her heel. Her trainers squeaked on the wet tiles all the way down to the French doors, but she didn't care. She swung through the conservatory, the designer kitchen, the hall. Mrs Hope caught up with her halfway down the drive.

'Sorry, Mum,' Mandy said, for being rude. But her mother didn't seem to mind as they marched out to the car, shoulder to shoulder.

'No good,' Mrs Hope sighed and opened the door.

Mandy sank back in the passenger seat. She felt bitter about spoilt little rich kids and their soft mothers. And she was panicking about the kittens. Two replies to their adverts so far, and two disastrous results! 'No, no good again!' she said.

Tears of disappointment threatened, but she bit them back. She had to carry on looking. She had to succeed!

Seven

The weekend was almost over, and still the kittens were homeless. Mr Williams would kick them out of his kitchen on Thursday, or do something dreadful. For him, they weren't creatures with feelings. They were just nuisances to be got rid of.

'That's how some people think,' Mandy's dad explained. 'Especially some older people round here. You don't get soft on animals when you live on farms or in the villages. When Mr Williams was young, they drowned unwanted kittens in the rain barrel behind the barn. I don't suppose they even thought it was cruel.'

Mandy shuddered. As far as she was concerned, it was murder.

'Come on, help me take this young chap along to Ernie's!' Mr Hope suggested. He picked up the plastic cage containing the baby squirrel. 'I've checked him over and he's as right as rain. He can go into the run at the back of Ernie's house and we'll see how he gets on.'

They set off on foot, down their lane to the main street. It was a sunny afternoon, with blossom everywhere. Gardeners were out with their trowels and pruners, making the flowers stand to attention. 'Good afternoon,' people said pleasantly. Some stopped to look at the squirrel and pass the time of day.

Mandy liked the fact that everyone knew her father. He'd been born up at Lilac Cottage and had lived in Welford all his life, except for his college days in York. The older villagers still called him 'young Adam' or 'Tom Hope's lad'. They knew he was a brainy boy, he'd been to college, and he was known as a decent vet. At any rate, he was one of them.

The women came out of their houses and made a fuss of Mandy, while the men described problems with moles on their lawns, or a sheep stuck in the cattle grid at the back of the Janekis' farm. The squirrel scampered in its cage, accepting offers of peanuts through the grille.

At last Mandy and her father reached the Fox and Goose. 'It's only taken us an hour and a quarter!' she remarked.

Mr Hope laughed and went into the pub for half a pint of beer and a can of cold Coke for Mandy. They spent another fifteen minutes in the last rays of sunshine, sitting on a bench, gossiping.

'Right!' Mr Hope wiped his beard clean of any stray froth and stood up. He sounded purposeful at last. 'You bring the squirrel, Mandy.'

She followed him across the cobbled courtyard of the pub. The squirrel scuttled in its cage.

'That used to be the forge,' Mr Hope said. He pointed to the plush restaurant at the side of the pub.

'I know, Dad, you've told me!'

He carried on regardless. 'My own grandfather had the place in the 1920s.'

'I know, Dad!' Boy, was he embarrassing sometimes. Mandy shuffled from one foot to the other. Soon she'd have to cycle over to Walton for the regular evening feed. The kittens were doing well on the special liquid food, and Walton herself was looking sleeker. Mandy was pleased with their progress. 'Come on, Dad, let's go!'

He turned and grinned. 'Sorry, love!' And he led the way again, down the side of the pub to a squashed up row of tiny two storey stone cottages that had seen better days. There were five cottages, all with beaten-up doors, unruly ivy and great stone slabs making a pathway along the length of the row. Most of the front doors stood open in the sunshine.

'Now then, young Adam!' a gruff voice said.

Mandy and Mr Hope stopped at the first house. She might have known they wouldn't make it to Ernie's without at least two more interruptions.

'Hello, Walter. Lovely day!' Mr Hope stopped and leaned in at Walter Pickard's door. 'How are things?'

'Mustn't grumble,' the old man said. 'Now then, young miss!'

Mandy smiled hello. Walter never remembered the name of anyone under thirty.

It was just 'young miss' or 'young sir'. He was a retired butcher, a Wednesday evening church bell-ringer alongside her grandad, and, what's more, a cat lover! Two lovely old ginger cats sunned themselves on his front doorstep.

'What have we here?' Walter said, bending and tapping the cage. Inside, the squirrel sat up and begged. 'Hey up!' Walter said, half laughing. He went off down the dark narrow hallway and came back with a piece of cream cracker which he fed to the squirrel.

Mandy liked Walter. He was a big man, but his deep voice was gentle, and his lined face under its flat cloth cap was always smiling. His wife had died last year, but Walter's three cats still kept him company. Mandy liked him because of his smile and his cats. What she couldn't understand was how he'd spent his entire working life in a butcher's shop. All those cold sides of beef hanging on their hooks. All those dead chickens. Mandy shuddered. She was glad she was a vegetarian. These days she hardly ever ate meat.

Mr Hope glanced at his watch. 'Do you know if Ernie's in?' he asked.

Walter nodded. 'Most likely.'

'In that case I'll just pop this little fellow along to him.' Mr Hope picked up the cage, saw Mandy was busy stroking the ginger cats and said, 'I'll leave you here, Mandy, to tell Walter the story of Ernie Bell and the orphan squirrel!' Then he wandered off down the row.

Mandy recounted the sad story of the squirrel.

'Ernie Bell!' Walter said, shaking his head. 'He's adopting a squirrel, that miserable old devil!' It was like saying he, Walter Pickard, had won the football pools.

Mandy had her hand deep in the soft warm fur of one of the old ginger cats when an idea struck her. She looked up from her cross-legged position on the path. 'Walter, how many cats have you got?' she asked casually. But the excitement of the idea was beginning to make her heart beat faster.

'Three,' he said. He sat down heavily on an old wooden stool just inside the doorway. 'That one's called Scraps because she feeds on any scraps I give her. She's not the least bit fussy.' He pointed to the one Mandy was stroking. 'And that's Missie over there, because she's a right little madam, and only eats the best fish and chicken breast.' This other ginger cat was contentedly purring in the sun. 'Then there's Tom. He's indoors at present.'

Mandy listened quietly, but she thought furiously,

'We used to have another one, mind,' Walter went on. 'My Mary loved cats, and it was her favourite, Susie, that passed away just after Christmas.' He sat with his own memories for a while, then pulled himself round. 'Susie was a dainty little cat, just like my Mary. That's why she was her favourite.' He smiled. 'Yes, indeed.'

Mandy nodded. She knew it was now or never. 'Why not get another?' she said. 'It just so happens I'm looking for homes for kittens right now, and there's one little dainty one, a little tortoiseshell called Amy, who'd be just right for you, I'm sure!'

Walter listened. He seemed to like the idea. 'A tortoiseshell?'

'Yes. They're only a few days old, and we're partly having to hand-rear them, James Hunter and me, because the mother's too weak. She was a stray. But we'll need homes for all of them.

Good homes!' She stressed the 'good' and looked up at Walter.

He blew out his cheeks like a trumpeter. 'A tortoiseshell?' he repeated. Mandy pictured a young kitten scampering about on the warm flagstones all summer long, jumping up at his wallflowers, tumbling in over the step.

'A really lovely little tortoiseshell!' she insisted. She held her breath.

'Aye, I'd love one,' Walter sighed.

'Oh, it'd be a perfect home for Amy!' Mandy told him. 'It's nice and quiet back here, off the road, and the older cats would look after her, and you know all about kittens. It would be ideal!'

Say yes, she prayed. *Say yes!*

But a shadow crept down the hallway. A big, butch bruiser of a shadow padding up to the doorstep in the sinister shape of Tom.

'Hello!' Mandy said to the barrel-shaped cat. He stood four-square in his doorway. He bared his teeth and hissed. 'Hello there!' She ran her fingers up and down the flagstones. 'Here then!' she coaxed. He ignored her game. Sulkily he padded across the step, back and forth, strong shouldered, wide mouthed. He was a

black and white bully with a pirate's black
patch over his left eye, a chewed left ear and
ragged whiskers.

'Ah, Tom!' Walter said with a sigh of regret.

Tom arched his back at Mandy and spat. He
padded around the two ginger females, just
checking up on them. Then he stood and stared
again at Mandy.

'There's Tom to consider, you see,' Walter
explained. 'Scraps and Missie would be fine.
But not Tom.' The old man shook his head.
'Just take one look at him. He'd eat a new kitten
for breakfast!'

Mandy could believe it. Never had she seen a
cat like Tom; a heavyweight, a bouncer, a sumo
wrestler of a cat!

'No,' Walter said sadly. 'Much as I'd like to, I'm afraid old Tom wouldn't be happy with a stranger about the place. You can see my problem?'

Mandy nodded. Though she was desperate, she had to agree.

'Never mind, Thomas, no one's going to come upsetting you.' Walter bent forward to scratch the chewed-up old ear. 'Just relax, old chap!'

The cat blinked and tilted its colossal head in victory. He'd staked out his territory and won.

Sadly Mandy got to her feet. Such a missed opportunity! But her dad was returning with the empty cage. 'Ready?' he asked.

They said their goodbyes to Walter and set off across the pub yard. The old man continued to sit on his stool, cats at his feet.

'I say,' Mr Hope said, glancing backwards, 'Old Walter's fond of cats. Why don't you—'

'It's all right, Dad,' Mandy interrupted, 'I already have. I asked him and he says he'd like another kitten, but Thomas the Terrible wouldn't appreciate it.' She joked, but she was feeling very low. 'In the end he said no.'

'Ah, well,' Mr Hope said, swinging the empty

cage, lost in his own thoughts.

All the gardeners had gone inside for tea, so their walk home was much quieter and quicker. Mrs Hope had prepared their own evening meal, knowing that Mandy would want to cycle over to school before it got dark. No one mentioned the kittens. If they had, Mandy felt she might have broken down. And her mum and dad knew when not to fuss. She ate, then packed her bag. She met James at the post office, and together they cycled to Walton.

Mr Williams was in a very bad mood.

'It's Sunday night,' Mrs Williams reminded them. 'He always gets like this on a Sunday night.'

He'd been stamping about the kitchen when they arrived, but as soon as he saw them, he grunted, took his Sunday newspaper and headed out of the room.

'It's because it's Monday tomorrow,' Mrs Williams explained. 'W-O-R-K! The dreaded four-letter word.'

Then Tuesday, then Wednesday, Mandy thought with a lurch. She wanted to stop the clock, or at least to stretch the days. The trouble was, as each visit to the kittens came and went, she grew fonder of them. They were about twelve centimetres long and weighed just 100 grams or so. They hadn't yet struggled to their feet and their eyes were still closed. Smoky was strongest, but Patch gave him a good scrap in their fight for food, while Amy and Eric were patient, more content.

Now was the time to ask Mrs Williams if they could gently tip the laundry basket on to its side so the kittens could begin to sniff the daylight of their own accord. 'And then Walton might be ready to move them to a new nest,' Mandy suggested.

'What, tip it over and leave it there?' Mrs Williams asked. She looked doubtful. 'It'd make the place look a terrible mess!' But in the end she agreed. The basket could be tipped on to its side.

As James and Mandy fed each of the kittens in turn, Mr Williams stamped back in. He was wearing a very clean, very stiff white shirt and a maroon tie. He looked smart in his dark suit, but he walked awkwardly, Mandy noticed for the first time. He frowned at the upturned laundry basket.

Mrs Williams leapt to her feet. She was ready for chapel, in her fawn dress and silk scarf. 'Now, Eric!' she warned. She saw him glaring at the two kittens who happened to be pulling by mistake at the sleeve of his best blue shirt. They were seeking out Walton, but getting tangled in the shirt instead. 'It's only till Wednesday night!' she promised.

He didn't even grunt. He just stamped out on to the porch.

'Good job it's Sunday!' Mrs Williams whispered.

'Why?' James asked.

'Eric never swears on a Sunday,' she said. She raised her eyebrows. 'Otherwise the air in the kitchen would be blue as that shirt!' She sighed as she picked up her shiny brown handbag. She checked her keys. 'Drop the latch as you go,' she reminded them. Then she followed her husband down the road to chapel.

Mandy shook her head. The kittens were all safe for the night. James was washing Walton's feeding bowl and saucer, and the mother cat was coming to Mandy for a final grateful stroke before she settled down with her kittens. 'I wish . . .' Mandy said. But she never finished the sentence.

James felt helpless too as they checked the kitchen, turned off the light and locked the door. 'That's what I like about computers,' he said out of the blue as they pulled up out of town on their bikes.

'Huh?' Mandy said. 'What are you talking about?' James sometimes came out with these odd things.

'Computers. That's what I like about them. They're straightforward and simple, and they never make you feel bad.'

'Not like people and animals, you mean?'

He nodded. 'And you can just switch them on and off, no problem.'

They cycled for a while in silence.

'But they go wrong!' Mandy objected. You shouldn't prefer machines to live things, surely.

'So do animals,' he said. Another silence. 'Like Benji.'

'Oh, what's wrong with Benji?' Mandy asked. James had had Benji for as long as she could remember; he was a lovely, docile black tomcat.

'Dunno,' James said. 'My mum has to bring

him into the Ark tomorrow morning to see if they can find out.'

Mandy nodded and sighed. 'Well, see you tomorrow, early?' she said by way of goodbye.

'Tomorrow early,' James promised, as they each rode their separate ways.

Eight

One little victory would be enough, Mandy thought. One home for one kitten. It wasn't asking much, and it would be a start. She went through the names they'd had so far, just to make sure that none of them would do.

Thinking hard, she passed Simon a thermometer to take the temperature of a Border collie who was just recovering from parvovirus. It was only because she was so young and strong that she'd survived.

Simon stroked the dog's long, black coat. 'At least they'll remember to have her vaccinated from now on,' he said.

Mandy nodded, but she was thinking of Miss Marjorie Spry. Surely even she could remember to open a tin of cat food each day. The kitten could be given a quiet, cosy corner in the garden shed if that old gardener would clear a space. Mandy stopped scooping meat into the dog bowls and stood, fork poised.

'A penny for them,' Simon said with a smile. He was looking at his watch.

'What?' Mandy was imagining Amy snugly tucked up behind the old flowerpots and garden shears.

'A penny for your thoughts!' Simon took the fork and carried on preparing bowls of food for their resident cocker spaniel and two black Labradors. 'You don't usually daydream on the job!' he said.

'Oh, sorry!' Mandy gave a sigh. Of course, The Riddings wasn't any good. Simon had broken her dream. She recalled the frozen snarl of the stuffed wildcat, the hopeful glass stare of the heron. All those dusty cases with dead animals in them. She feared it would never work to send Amy there, and the poor kitten was still homeless.

'Best get a move on,' Simon said. 'Here, you

do the hamster dishes next, while I clean out the cages. And remember Flopsy and Co. out at the back!'

Mandy took the scoop full of rabbit food out into the back garden. There was always the Parker Smythe mansion for Smoky, she told herself. She knew she was clutching at straws, though. How long would it be before the kitten lost its novelty? Two days? Mandy sighed again. And that was only if Imogen would accept a grey cat. No, she wouldn't wish Imogen Parker Smythe on her worst enemy, let alone on precious Smoky.

If only Walter Pickard's old tomcat had been better tempered! Mandy stood there with a handful of oats and sunflower seed mixture, deep in thought.

When she went inside, Simon had finished the hamster cages. He took a last look at her, and in his quiet way took charge. 'Look,' he said, 'I'll finish here. I thought you had to get off to school early again.'

'What? Oh, yes, thanks!' Mandy dusted down her hands and scrambled out of her white coat. 'Is that the time? I must dash!'

She was out of Animal Ark and in her school

uniform when she bumped into her mum on the stairs. 'Any phone calls?' she asked, hoping for more responses to the adverts.

'No,' Mrs Hope said.

'Right.' She hadn't really expected any this time. Her hopes were not high.

Then she was out of the house, up the lane to meet James outside McFarlane's. Her mind was still working overtime. *I suppose I could always try Walter again*, she thought as she screeched to a halt. James was already there.

'Sorry I'm late!' she said.

James was quieter than usual as they cycled over, but Mandy had a lot on her mind, too.

School went by in a semi-daze. She got two questions wrong in history, and a telling off from Mr Holmes. 'What's wrong, Amanda? This isn't like you. Been watching too much television, I expect. Now just pay attention, please!' Mandy went red and hot, and tried to concentrate.

She was thinking of the kittens when a group of friends asked her if she was going to the disco on Friday. Mandy didn't answer. 'Oh, be like that!' one said. They were all giggling about something or other. 'Don't think we care whether you come or not! You're not the centre of the universe, Mandy Hope!' And they flounced off.

Mandy shrugged. It was time to go and feed the kittens.

And she was still thinking of them when James came up after school and told her quietly that he had to go straight home tonight. He'd promised his mum specially.

Mandy nodded. 'See you tomorrow then,' she said. She had a plan in her head; not much of a plan, but she'd decided she would visit Walter again. She'd feed the kittens first, then she'd call in at the cottages. Anyway, it couldn't do any harm. She'd invent an excuse; maybe she'd visit Ernie Bell's squirrel and just 'happen' to call in on Walter. He mustn't think she was pestering on purpose.

'Hello, young miss!' Walter greeted her from his open door. 'Where's that grandad of yours got to? I've not seen him round here lately.'

Mandy propped her bike against the end wall. 'Hi, Walter.' She tried to sound casual. 'He's off touring in his new van.' She gave him one of her cheeriest smiles. It was an effort, but she wanted to be bright and breezy.

'Camping!' Walter said with a low whistle. 'At their age!'

'Not exactly.' She explained the luxuries of the modern mobile home. 'It has a fridge, electricity, everything!'

'Hmph! Don't they have a fridge and electricity at their house, then?'

'Yes.'

'Well, then, what's the point?' Walter said. His ginger cats came padding elegantly down the hall.

Mandy gave in and changed the subject. She stroked Scraps and Missie. 'I've just popped by to see Mr Bell's squirrel,' she said casually. 'To see if he's settled in OK.'

Walter nodded. 'Aye, if he'll see you,' he said. 'Ernie doesn't always answer his door!'

'I'll be back in a minute,' she said.

She walked up the flagged path to the end of the row. She knocked hard. The green door was faded and flaking; it needed a good coat of paint. And it had an old lion knocker which hadn't been cleaned for years. It was stiff with disuse. She knocked again.

'Hold your horses, hold your horses!' Ernie

grumbled from inside. She heard bolts sliding, locks turning. Finally, Ernie opened his front door.

Mandy heard Walter mumble and turn back inside his own house. She was left to face Ernie alone.

'Yes?' Ernie snapped. He was a small man with a shock of straight white hair rising back from his lined forehead. There was something birdlike about his sharp nose, his bright, dark eyes. He wore an old waistcoat and a shirt without a collar. 'Yes?' he said again, peering at Mandy.

She introduced herself as the vet's daughter. 'My dad brought back the squirrel yesterday. How is he?' she asked.

Ernie frowned. 'Fine, fine. What do you want now? You can't have him back, you know. I've paid the bill!'

'No, I don't want to take him back,' Mandy tried to explain.

'Good. It cost me a fortune just to have him checked over, I can tell you. But I paid!' he insisted. He stood there, frowning.

'No, I—' Mandy hesitated, then changed tactics. 'What's his name?' she asked.

Ernie paused. 'Sammy,' he said, as if he didn't want anyone to hear. 'All right?'

'Yes, it's a nice name. I was just wondering, could I take a look at him, please?'

She waited until Ernie made up his mind. He stared at her, thought a while, then nodded. 'This way,' he said at last.

He led her down a dark passage, through his kitchen and out into the backyard. Four gardens along the way, Walter was out in his garden. He leant his forearms against his fence top. 'Now then, Ernie!' he greeted his unfriendly neighbour.

Ernie grunted. He stood by, watching suspiciously as Mandy inspected the squirrel run.

'Sammy!' Mandy called gently. There was a sturdy hutch at the far end of the run, with a small hole for an entrance, which only something as tiny and agile as a squirrel could use. The little creature poked out its round grey head.

'Here,' Ernie said. 'Tempt him with these!' He handed Mandy a few peanuts from his trouser pocket.

And Sammy bounded out of the hutch. He

clung upside-down to the netting, swinging like a trapeze artist towards her. His feet never touched the ground.

Mandy held out the nuts in the palm of her hand. Delicately Sammy watched, reached out a paw and snatched the food. He swung away to a safe distance, then nibbled.

Mandy studied him. This was only the second time she'd been this close to a squirrel. The run was ten metres long, made of timber and fine mesh. Very safe. 'This is great!' she told Ernie, tapping the framework.

'Hmm.' Ernie nodded. 'So it should be.' He too was watching the squirrel, and his face had lost its frown. 'I've had a fair bit of practice, mind you. I was a carpenter for more than fifty years!' Then as if he'd given away top secret information, his mouth clamped shut and the frown returned.

'Well, it's great,' Mandy said. 'Really sturdy and safe. I'm glad Sammy's found such a good home!' It was almost enough to take her mind off homeless kittens. But she could see Walter along there in his own yard, and she was desperate to talk with him. She remembered her real purpose: to persuade Walter and old

Tom to change their minds. 'Can I come and visit Sammy again?' she asked Ernie.

He swallowed hard, but he nodded slowly. 'You can call again,' he agreed. 'It might not always suit me to answer the door, you understand. But you can always try.'

He followed her out to the front of the house. 'Well, Mr Bell!' Mandy was about to turn and thank him again for showing her the squirrel, but the flaky green door was already closed. And like a figure in a Swiss cuckoo clock, Walter was already out at his own front door. As usual, he was not minding his own business.

Mandy wandered towards him. She was going to ask, 'How's old Tom today?' and then gently add the idea that perhaps Tom would take to a new kitten, if they introduced him to the idea gradually.

But Walter must have been a mind-reader. She never got any further than 'How's old Tom?' before he cut her short.

'It's no good you wheedling away, young miss!' Walter laughed at her surprise. 'I know what you're going to ask, and Tom's answer is still no!'

As if to confirm this, Tom came bowling

round the corner at top speed and bashed straight into Mandy's bike. Down it crashed. Tom wailed loudly, leapt the spinning wheels, and vanished across the pub yard.

'See!' Walter said, laughing again. He picked up the bike. 'Nothing's safe with our Tom on the scene!' He turned to Mandy, then he looked down the row to Ernie's end house. 'But you know something, I think we've just had an idea!'

'We have?' To Mandy it didn't feel as if anything was going right.

'Yes. You hit it off with old Ernie, didn't you?' Walter scratched his head; a sure sign that he was thinking.

'I suppose so,' Mandy said doubtfully. 'Listen, you don't think I should ask him!' Her eyes lit up. 'I mean, you mean I should ask him to take a kitten!' She felt the idea light up all the dark corners of her mind.

But Walter was shaking his head. 'No, no, I don't think you should ask him exactly!'

Mandy's face fell again. 'Why not? He likes animals. He rescued little Sammy, didn't he?'

'Yes, but Ernie would say no if you asked him directly. On principle, he always says no. He's a grumpy, cantankerous old so-and-so, is Ernie.'

Mandy had to agree. 'So what's our idea?' she asked.

'It's this!' Walter got into a huddle with Mandy round the corner, out of sight.

The idea involved taking a very big risk. But then Mandy had forty-eight hours to solve four very big problems. She listened to Walter, she nodded, she considered it. She thought of Sammy snug in his custom-built hutch. She decided to risk it.

So she rang home and said she'd be late. Then she rode back over to Walton.

Mrs Williams watched with concern as Mandy gave Amy a special feed and tucked her into a specially lined cardboard box. Amy peered up, unseeing, sniffed, then settled down. Walton came over, glanced in, looked up at Mandy, then retreated to the laundry basket. She sat quietly inside with her other three kittens, looking out.

'She trusts you!' Mrs Williams said. 'Poor lamb, she trusts you with her babies!'

Mandy nodded. It was a hard thing to do, to take the kitten from her mother, but it was a hard thing Mr Williams was threatening to do, and Walter's plan made it necessary. 'Good girl, Walton,' she said. Carefully she folded down the flaps of the cardboard box.

'I hope you know what you're doing!' Mrs Williams whispered.

Mandy looked her in the face. Her heart was in her mouth as she nodded and went outside. She strapped the box on to her bike, nodded again at Mrs Williams, tried not to think about Walton and the three cosy kittens in their basket, and set off across the moor.

It was the most heartstopping bike ride she'd ever made. Every bend, every hill she took at snail's pace. She came down into Welford holding her breath. She stopped at the pub, out of sight of Walter and Ernie's row of cottages. Then she unstrapped the box and crept with it in through Walter's open door.

'Got it?' Walter asked.

Mandy nodded. She opened the box. Amy mewed at the light. 'Are you sure this will work?' she asked again.

Walter's head went to one side. 'Not sure,' he said 'Not one hundred per cent.' He gazed down at tiny, helpless Amy. 'She's just a skinny little thing!' He tickled her head.

'Ernie's got a mind of his own. You can bet he'll do exactly the opposite to what you ask. Always has. You say to him, "Ernie, do me a favour, fix the latch on this back gate for me," and he'll say straight back, "What do you think I am, the odd-jobman round here?" and he'll stamp off in the other direction. But if he thinks it's his idea and he sees your gate's broken, he'll make a point of coming up and he'll say, "I saw your latch needed mending, Walter, so I just got out my toolbag and fixed it for you." Just like that!'

Mandy understood. 'Like rescuing Sammy, you mean? It had to be his idea.' She lifted Amy out of her box. 'So if he finds a tiny kitten abandoned on his doorstep, he'll take her in?'

Walter nodded. 'As long as he does think it's his idea! Then he'll want to keep her and look after her, just like the squirrel. He'll come along to me for advice because he knows I've got the three cats, and I'll suggest, very cunning, how much better it'd be to find a feeding mother until the kitten's properly on its feet. That's where you come in, little miss!'

Mandy looked hard at Amy. 'Are you sure?'

He nodded again. 'Ernie's got a heart of gold, underneath it all!' Walter smiled. 'Go on, lass, what have you got to lose? That kitten will have a foster home and be back with her mother before you can say Jack Robinson!'

So Mandy took the precious bundle down the length of the row. Amy squirmed in her hands, mewing piteously. 'Shh!' she whispered. Could she do it? Mandy felt as if her heart would stop. Could she leave the poor little thing on a cold doorstep?

She almost stopped to retrace her steps. But what was the alternative? She had less than two days left. Forcing herself to go on, she stooped down by Ernie's front doorstep. She closed her eyes, backed away, and fled down to Walter's house.

'Now we just have to wait,' Walter said. They stood inside his doorway, listening to Amy's tiny wail.

'Oh, quick!' Mandy breathed. 'Please hear her and come quickly!'

But Ernie's door stayed shut.

Amy mewed her high-pitched sound. Would he hear it? They waited. Mandy leaned forward, desperately wanting to see if Amy was all right.

But Walter pulled her back. 'You mustn't let him see you!' he warned.

The wait seemed endless. Minutes went by. Amy's tiny howling continued.

Then finally they heard the metal bolts of Ernie's door. They heard the latch turn. The door scraped open. 'What the—!' Ernie said. He grunted as he stooped. 'Oh-aagh!' They heard him sigh as he picked up the kitten and straightened his old back. He stepped out on to the path. He took time to look up and down. He even carried Amy a few steps towards Walter's house, then he turned and went indoors, carrying the kitten.

'Well?' Mandy was still holding her breath. She looked at Walter.

Walter listened. He considered carefully. Then he brought up one hand in a thumbs-up sign. 'I reckon it's worked!' he said.

They had to wait half an hour, maybe more, drinking tea and eating Rich Tea biscuits, before they heard Ernie shuffling down the path to Walter's door.

'Say nothing!' Walter warned. 'And stay here!'

Mandy nodded.

'Now then, Walter,' Ernie said. He poked his head inside the front door. 'You know about cats!'

'I do, Ernie,' Walter said. 'I know something about them, any rate.' Mandy sat out of sight in the back kitchen as Walter went down the hall to greet Ernie. 'Why, what have you got there?' He managed to sound genuinely surprised.

'Kitten,' Ernie said. 'What's it look like?' He had wrapped Amy in an old grey jumper. 'It's shivering.' He showed the little bundle to Walter.

'Aye, it would,' Walter said. 'It's only a littl'un.'

'It just turned up out of the blue,' Ernie said. 'I was just doing my washing-up when I heard it set up a racket on my doorstep! I reckon its mother dropped it there; one too many to look after in the litter!'

'Well, it must be your week for it,' Walter said, keeping his voice flat this time. 'First the squirrel, now this.'

'I dunno about that. It just turned up.' Ernie stood there looking helpless. Peeping, Mandy could see the two old men, head to head against the square of light in the doorway.

'Ah, well, I reckon you'll have to get rid of this one,' Walter said. 'Two orphans to look after is more than you can manage.'

Mandy gasped and bit her lip. How could he? How could Walter take such a risk?

But Ernie gave Walter his eagle stare. 'What do you mean, more than I can manage?' He wrapped Amy up carefully. 'I've no intention of getting rid of it, Walter Pickard! No, this little kitten is here to stay!'

Mandy cried. She cried tears of silent joy.

'Aye, but how will you feed it? Look at it, poor little scrap. It needs feeding already,' Walter insisted.

Ernie thought about this for a while. 'That's why I'm coming to you, Walter. You know about cats.'

Now it was Walter's turn to stand there looking awkward and sullen. 'It's too young for me to handle. It needs a mother cat,' he said. 'One that's still feeding her own youngsters.'

Ernie squared his shoulders and asked how they would set about finding such a thing; a mother cat that would feed his kitten until it was weaned? He'd like Walter to ring the vet right then and there, on his telephone, and get the vet's young girl over there as quick as possible. 'I reckon she'll know of just such a cat,' Ernie said, hugging Amy to his chest.

'Oh, she'll know,' Walter confirmed, giving a little smile.

Back in the kitchen, Mandy grinned. Walter's plan had worked perfectly!

'Then you go ahead and give her a ring. You tell her I want her down at my cottage in fifteen minutes sharp!' Ernie instructed. 'And tell her to bring something to carry a tiny kitten in. We need a mother cat straight off, else my little kitten will starve to death!'

'Right!' Walter agreed.

'Right!' And Ernie marched on back home with Amy.

Walter came back grinning all over his face.

Mandy sat on the kitchen stool and smiled through her tears. They'd found a home for Amy. At last they'd found one good home!'

Nine

Mandy paid a visit to Ernie's, complete with her lined cardboard box. She fed Amy quickly and expertly, mixing the powdered food in a miniature feeding bottle. She held Amy in one hand, then stroked her abdomen with a forefinger to help her digest the food and get rid of the waste. Ernie didn't bat an eyelid at that.

'You have to do it, otherwise, they hang on to it and get constipated,' Mandy explained. 'That's why the mother cats lick them.'

'And how often will this mother cat have to feed it?'

'*She* needs feeding every couple of hours. And the mother will keep her warm too,' Mandy said.

Ernie picked up his kitten and said an awkward goodbye. His fingers looked broad and clumsy against Amy's tiny head, but he held her calmly. He gave her every scrap of his attention. He bent his white head, making encouraging little chucking noises with his tongue. Then he looked up. 'I'll call her Tiddles!' he said.

Mandy started to protest, then bit her tongue hard. She couldn't tell Ernie that Amy already had a name. She swallowed and nodded. 'Good idea.' She took the kitten from Ernie and put her carefully in the box. 'She'll be ready to come home in six or seven weeks,' she promised.

So Amy became Tiddles. 'Brilliant name, isn't it?' She greeted James with the news when they met up in the village early next morning. But Mandy was so thrilled that the name hardly mattered. 'Three more to go!' she said, full of new enthusiasm for the task. The morning was sunny. Things had begun to go right.

James nodded. He was looking pale and tired.

'What's wrong?' Mandy asked. She was peering in through the post office window to make sure that their card was still up there on the notice-board.

'Nothing.' James shook his head, and made ready to set off for school. He refused to look Mandy in the face as he mumbled, 'Let's go.'

'No, there is something wrong!' Mandy insisted. James was always shy and only ever got visibly excited about football. But today there was something making him even quieter than usual. He hadn't really reacted to the news about Amy. He hadn't said, Great. Well done. I knew you could do it, Mandy!

James shook his head again. He was staring down at his trainers.

Mandy put one hand on the handlebar of his bike. 'It's Benji, isn't it?' she said softly.

And James nodded.

'Oh, James, what's wrong with him?' She could have kicked herself. She'd been so full of her own news that she'd forgotten all about poor Benji being ill.

But James couldn't speak. He just sighed.

'He's going to be all right, isn't he? I mean they'll sort him out down at the Ark. It isn't anything serious, is it? What did my mum and dad say?' Mandy was beginning to sense something really awful. She'd never seen James look so sad.

And finally he came out with it. 'Benji's dead,' he said. 'We had to have him put down.'

Mandy gasped. She expected the whole sky to come crashing down. Benji was dead. 'Why?' She couldn't believe it.

The story came pouring out now. 'He had some kind of tumour on his brain. We didn't know it was anything serious, only over the weekend he was a bit groggy. Off his food and so on.' James paused to take a deep breath. 'He kept staggering. My dad laughed and said he must have been out on Saturday night drinking. He looked pretty sorry for himself, so my mum said we'd take him into the Ark.' He paused again and glanced at Mandy. 'I think my mum knew,' he said.

She nodded. 'Then what?' No more Benji, she was thinking. No more Benji curled up on a seat in the Hunters' conservatory. No more Benji leaping from the sloping roof up through the bathroom window. Benji had always been there. He was part of the Hunter family.

James shrugged. He stared hard at his feet again. He was standing astride his bike, head down, miserable. 'My mum took him in yesterday. By that time he could hardly stand. It was your mum who looked at him.' Mandy realised that nothing in James's life had ever been so difficult for him to say. 'Anyway, she said he had this growth on his brain. And there was nothing to be done in this kind of case.'

'So?'

He sniffed. 'So your mum explained that he'd be in a lot of pain.'

'And *your* mum agreed to have him put to sleep?'

James nodded. 'It would have been cruel to let him live.'

For a second Mandy's hand touched James's. 'That's true,' she said.

Then there was a big silence. They both thought of Benji. Patient old Benji who'd grown up with them, who'd always let you pick him up any old how, and who always sat on your lap and let you tickle his chin. He'd put up over the years with all their rough treatment, and he'd never put in a cross word. He was a great cat.

'Let's go!' James said. He glanced round at

Mandy. 'I told my mum to tell them at the Ark not to say anything to you about it. I wanted to tell you myself.'

Mandy nodded and followed on. Life, like the road over to Walton, was full of ups and downs.

It must have been hard for James, she thought, to help with the kittens this morning. He did the jobs as usual, before school and during lunch break. He listened as Mandy told Mrs Williams how Amy, alias Tiddles, was safely back with Walton. And her future was secure.

'I hope this Ernie Bell person knows what he's doing with this kitten!' Mrs Williams said primly. 'I mean, men! They don't know how to look after things properly. They're not made that way!'

Mandy raised her eyebrows and glanced at James. He was busy with Smoky's feed. 'Oh, I don't know about that,' she said.

'Not my Eric, at least,' Mrs Williams blundered on. 'Mind you, he's a bit old-fashioned in that respect.'

As if on cue, Mr Williams tramped in for his lunch. He ate in silence, glancing sullenly at the kitten activity in the far corner of the kitchen. 'Tomorrow's D-Day!' he reminded them as he reached for his cap. 'And don't you forget!'

D-Day. Death Day. Destruction Day. Deadline Day. Mandy didn't think it was possible to hate someone as much as she hated Mr Williams just then. He stamped off down the garden path, tweaking a rose bush, perking up a primula.

'He's got to go and see the Headmaster!' Mrs Williams whispered to Mandy. 'He's had the summons!'

Mandy raised her head. She couldn't help that, she thought. And all she really cared about right now was the kitten problem.

'Do you want to go straight on home after school?' she asked James, on their way into afternoon lessons. She thought there was only so much she could ask him to do, considering Benji.

James looked up at the school shield in the entrance hall. Underneath there was a list of names of men who'd died in two wars, and underneath that was the school motto: 'Through Suffering We Succeed!'

'No,' he said to Mandy. 'I'll be there as usual!'

* * *

James must have been thinking about poor Benji all through his games afternoon. Mandy had glanced out of the science lab window down on to the sports field, and she'd spotted him hanging about miserably on the touchline, most unlike him.

But when they met up after school, his face looked composed, even calm. 'I just want to ring my mum,' he told her. 'I'll be across in a minute.'

So Mandy went on ahead. As usual, the routine of caring for the kittens took over and she managed to push away the worry about James. She watched with delight their fluffy, wriggling little bodies, their ears beginning to unfold and perk up into position, their bruising battle to feed and to survive.

James came in just as she lifted Eric out of the basket for his feed. She handed the kitten to him. 'Here, you do Eric,' she said.

They worked in silence for a few minutes. Then James pushed his glasses up the bridge of his nose, sat back and made an announcement. 'I'd like Eric!' He said it quite straightforwardly, just like, 'I'd like a Mars bar!' or, 'Tea with milk but no sugar, please!'

Mandy stared. 'What did you say?'

'I'd like Eric,' he repeated. 'I've thought about it, and I'd like to adopt Eric!'

'Are you sure?' Mandy put Smoky back into the basket. 'I mean you're sure it's not too soon after . . . I mean, well, are you *sure?*'

'Yes. I rang my mum. She agrees. If we're going to get another cat after Benji, we should do it straight away.' He looked down, half sad, half happy at the new scrap of life on his lap. 'And I'm sure Benji wouldn't mind!'

Mandy waltzed around the kitchen. 'Oh, great!' she said. 'You hear that, Walton? Oh, brilliant! Oh, James!' She smiled and smiled.

Walton mewed.

There were practical things to arrange. When Mr Williams threw the kittens out next day, should James take Eric home then, or could they work out a way to keep Walton and the kittens together until they were weaned? A halfway house. That was the thing to work on, Mandy told James. She looked at Mrs Williams, who was hovering in the doorway with her shopping basket.

'Don't ask me!' she muttered darkly. 'Eric is

in with the Headmaster this very minute. Lord knows what's going to happen to any of us!' She went out tight-lipped, shaking her head.

'It's something we can work on,' Mandy told James as they went out to their bicycles. 'A halfway house. Anyway, we've got two good homes. Two brilliant homes!' Mandy could have sung for joy as they rode home.

'Two to go!' Mandy told her mum as she flung her schoolbag in the corner of the hallway. She told her about James's decision to take Eric. 'He's probably the grumpiest kitten of them all, like the person he's named after,' she joked. 'But James seems to like him!'

Mrs Hope smiled. 'He's a good boy.' Then she asked Mandy to help in the kitchen. 'Your dad's out on an emergency call. One of Mrs Janeki's sheep. But your grandad rang while you were out, just to let us know they're back.'

Mandy nodded. 'Did they have a good time?'

'He didn't say. But he said your gran had got a reply from the Prime Minister.' Mrs Hope looked puzzled. 'Could that be right?'

'Yes. But that was quick.' Mandy asked if she

could run up to see them.

'After supper,' Mrs Hope said. She always had to remind her daughter to slow down enough to eat. 'What's the point of me preparing all these vegetarian meals for you if you won't even sit down and eat one!' she complained.

Mandy gave her a hug. 'OK, Mum, after supper!'

The camper van sat in the driveway, splashed but splendid. 'Hi, Gran! Hi, Grandad!' Mandy burst in on them. She reported the good news about Tiddles ('What a name!') and Eric. She said James was a hero, a real hero!

'Oho!' her grandad raised his eyebrows.

'No, Grandad, not like that!' she said.

'That's what they always say. I think Mandy's got a soft spot for young James.'

'Stop teasing, Thomas!' Mandy's gran warned. 'Anyway, she's come to see my letter from the Prime Minister, haven't you, love!'

Mandy nodded and laughed. 'Sorry, Gran. It's just that the kittens have been taking up all my time. Did you have a good holiday?' she remembered to ask.

There was a small silence. 'Yes,' Gran said.

'But about this letter from 10 Downing Street. See, official notepaper!' She waved the reply in Mandy's face.

'"Yes" means "Yes, but!",' Grandad put in. 'And then we quickly change the subject!'

'Why, what happened? Did the camper break down?'

'Break down!' he exclaimed. 'You must be joking!'

'Of course not,' Mrs Hope said. 'The camper was perfect. But Scarborough wasn't.'

'Not sunny?'

'Sodden,' Mrs Hope conceded. 'Forty-two hours of solid rain. We counted!'

'Ah,' Mandy said. 'What a shame.'

'Yes, but this letter here, see!' Gran waved it before starting to read:

'"Dear Mrs Hope,
The Prime Minister acknowledges receipt of your letter. While he recognises your concern about the continued existence of your local sub post office, he wishes me to point out that Government policy on **the issue is the concern of one of his junior ministers.**

Accordingly he has asked me to pass on
this matter to the relevant department.
                    Yours sincerely,
                    E.B. Whyte
                    (Assistant private secretary
                        to the Prime Minister)"

'There!' Mrs Hope flung the cream-coloured
letter on to the table.

'What does it mean?' Mandy asked. 'Are they
going to close McFarlane's or not?'

'It doesn't mean yes, it doesn't mean no. It
doesn't mean anything!' Gran said indignantly.

'It means they've passed the buck,' Grandad
said. 'As usual.'

'They won't get away with it!' Gran insisted.

Grandad muttered in a stage whisper, 'Watch
it, love, she's on the warpath!'

Gran ignored him. 'We'll have a campaign.
Save our post office!' She stood up and strode
across the room.

Mandy was enjoying this; her gran on her
high horse.

'I'll have to organise everything, of course!'
There was a glint in Gran's eye.

Bells began to ring in Mandy's head. In fact,

they set up a giant racket! Did this mean her grandparents would have to put their feet firmly back on Welford ground?

'This'll take a lot of time and energy, Gran,' she pointed out.

'Who cares?' Gran swept around the room. 'It's important! In fact, it's vital! We'll design a logo for our campaign. A heart shape, to show our post office is at the heart of the village!' Her hair was coming loose from its comb and she was looking very fiery.

'I'm glad I'm not the poor little Prime Minister!' Grandad laughed.

'Does this mean you might not go to Portugal?' Mandy asked. 'I mean, you might have to stay at home more to run this campaign.'

Gran stopped in her paces. Grandad said, 'Ha!'

'We-ell,' Gran said. 'We might not go quite so far afield as we thought.' She gave Mandy a little grin. 'The fact is, we missed you all terribly; you and your mum and dad, and this old place!' She sighed. 'We're a pair of old softies, after all!'

'And then there's my tomatoes to consider,' Grandad said thoughtfully. 'I'll have to talk nicely to my tomatoes!'

Mandy looked at them, bursting to put the question. She took a great, deep breath. 'Does this mean you might be willing to take a kitten after all?'

They broke into smiles, both of them. They hugged her. 'We thought you'd never ask!' They looked at each other. Clearly they'd been thinking about it all the time they'd been away in soggy Scarborough.

'Smoky!' Mandy said, breathless.

'On two conditions,' Gran added.

'What?' She glowed with happiness. A home for the third kitten. A home just up the hill from Animal Ark. Mandy couldn't believe it.

'First, you've got to agree to come up and feed him whenever we do go away for a couple of days,' Gran said. 'When we go off in the camper to lovely Llandudno or wherever.'

This was hardly a condition! Mandy nodded, speechless. She'd love to feed Smoky. Then he'd be half hers, wouldn't he! She just sat there nodding.

'Second!' Grandad said, frowning and trying to look serious. 'You must swear to water my tomatoes!'

'Oh, yes,' she said. She'd even talk to them. 'Oh, yes, yes!'

Ten

Thursday came, and Mandy woke three quarters happy, one quarter sad. Her heart felt pulled apart over Patch; poor little Patch, the only kitten still left homeless.

Mrs Hope looked at her across the breakfast table. 'Problem?' she asked.

'You realise what day it is,' Mandy said miserably.

'Thursday,' her father said helpfully over the top of his newspaper.

'Yes, Thursday. And I've found homes for three of the kittens in Mr Williams's kitchen, but there's still one left over! Today's the deadline!' The word 'deadline' had an awful hollow ring.

'Hasn't the mother cat decided to move off to a new nest site yet?' Mr Hope asked.

Mandy shook her head. 'No, she's still there in the kitchen, in the laundry basket. And today's the day *he* throws them out!'

'You mean Mr Williams,' Mrs Hope corrected her. 'Not "he". So what next?'

'Gran and Grandad say they don't mind if the kittens and Walton move in with them until the kittens are weaned in about six weeks time.' Mandy managed a smile of relief. It had been a close thing all round.

'But?' Mrs Hope asked.

'But they say the same thing as you. They say I have to find a home for Patch. Otherwise it's cruel to keep him alive!' Her eyes filled. 'Poor Patch!'

'It's true. You can't just turn him out to fend for himself when the time comes. He has to have a home!' Even her soft-hearted father was telling her the same thing; the thing she didn't want to hear.

'Dad!' she cried.

'There's no "Dad!" about it,' Mrs Hope said

firmly. 'Look, Mandy, you've done brilliantly to find these three homes. We think you're wonderful!'

'Don't!' The tears brimmed over and down her cheeks.

Mrs Hope looked across at Mr Hope. Mandy thought she spied a glimmer of hope through her tears. 'Listen, love, I'll come across and see you at school this lunchtime, all right?'

'What for?' Mandy said, sniffing and drying her eyes.

'Wait and see. I can't promise anything yet.' Mrs Hope smiled and patted Mandy's hand. 'Just wait and see.'

That lunchtime Mandy fed Patch with an aching heart. James was busy with little Eric, and the other two kittens were already snuggled down in the basket, when there was a knock at the door.

'Hello. Is Mandy here?' a voice said to Mrs Williams.

She recognised her mum, but the misery of looking down at Patch's little face, his eyes nearly open now, was too much. She couldn't bear to think about what might have to happen to him.

'Mandy?' her mum's voice said again.

She looked up.

'I've brought someone with me. Mrs Hope was gentle but firm, as always. 'Come in, and let's have a look at this little fellow.'

Mandy felt suddenly surrounded by people and dragged back to the present from fears of the future. She pulled herself together. 'Sorry,' she said, standing up with Patch cupped in her hands. Her eyes focused on the visitors: Miss Marjorie and Miss Joan Spry!

What on earth was Mrs Hope up to? Mandy stood up, ready to protest, but her mum gave her a meaningful look.

'This is the kitten Mandy came to see you about,' Mrs Hope explained calmly. 'And I'm sure she apologises for running off so rudely.' She smiled encouragingly at Mandy, who went red and nodded without saying anything.

The two sisters nodded back and peered down at Patch. They poked their thin faces towards him curiously. They looked silently at each other.

Mandy had got over her shock. She trusted

her mum to know what she was doing. And today the Spry twins didn't look so strange. Their untidy hair was combed back underneath straw hats, and their pastel summer coats made them look like quaint wedding guests.

'This is the only kitten left without a home,' Mandy said. She offered Patch to one of the twins, not knowing which one.

The twin shook her head. 'No, give him to Joan. See if she likes him,' Miss Marjorie said. 'She did promise to try and like him!'

Mandy held out the kitten again. With shaking hands Miss Joan took the little fur scrap and cradled it. She brought her face close to the kitten's and felt it lick her finger. 'What is its name?' she breathed.

'Patch,' Mandy said, holding her own breath. 'He's just one week old!'

Joan looked up at her sister. The silence held them all like a net. Would she say yes? Would she give Patch a home and a future?

'Yes,' she said at last. 'I think I like him!'

'Of course you do! What did I tell you!' Miss Marjorie said.

And they all smiled and congratulated one another. They listened to Mandy's instructions about how a kitten should be treated: 'Don't poke him, don't press him too hard, don't disturb him too much!' She said they should put him back with his mother now. 'The excitement's too much for him,' she said as she returned a squeaking Patch to his warm, dark nest.

The Spry twins smiled and thanked Mandy and went off happily through the porch, arm in arm.

'See!' Mrs Hope said, head to one side. 'Didn't I say they were harmless? You have to learn that all people are different, but that doesn't make them wrong. This kitten will be the best thing that's happened to the twins in an awfully long time!'

Mandy laughed and hugged her mum. 'Oh, thanks!' she said. A great weight had lifted off her chest. She sighed and looked in on the kittens. They were curled up, snug and warm against Walton's sleeping body. 'Four homes! We did it!'

'*You* did it,' Mrs Hope said. 'You and James!'

They looked at each other with huge grins on their faces. James went red, even before Mandy hugged him.

When Miss Marjorie came back in for a moment, James leapt back. Dainty as a canary in her pale yellow coat, she made straight for Mandy. 'Thank you, my dear!' she said, patting her hand. 'Thank you for bringing life back into our dark, dreary house. It's all due to you!' She beamed, nodded lightly at James. 'I'd best get back to my sister. We'll wait for you in the car,' she told Mrs Hope before tripping off again.

'Happy now?' Mandy's mum asked.

Her eyes shone with tears again. She nodded and they nearly spilled over. This time Mandy could say nothing at all!

Afternoon school ended and the great move began. 'It's time for a new nest, Walton,' Mandy told her gently. 'And you don't even have to do it yourself, you lucky cat!'

'You're sure it'll be all right now?' Mrs Williams fussed. There was no sign of her husband. It was a heavy day, threatening rain when Mandy's grandparents' camper van pulled up in the playground. 'Walton won't desert these kittens now?' She stood at the kitchen sink, grasping a tea towel.

'No, it'll work out OK, Mrs Williams. Don't worry!' Mandy looked up and realised the old lady would miss Walton and the kittens after all. She smiled. 'Honestly, Walton would fight to the death for them now. She's made a good strong bond with them. Thanks to you, of course!'

'Oh!' Mrs Williams raised her hands and smiled modestly.

'Yes, you gave them a good start. Now my gran and grandad will keep a close eye on them up at Lilac Cottage!'

'Then what?' Mrs Williams folded her tea towel into a precise rectangle. She laid it down on the draining-board and smoothed it carefully.

'Then James will take Eric and give him a home,' Mandy said, handing the kitten to him.

'And me and my wife will keep this little chap,' Grandad said, lifting Smoky in one hand.

'Ernie Bell is waiting to have Amy – er – Tiddles. And now Patch has found a home at The Riddings!' Mandy counted them off on her fingers.

Mrs Williams sniffed and nodded. 'And what about Walton?'

Mandy looked at James. 'We haven't got that far!'

He shrugged. 'We've got a bit of time to sort it out.'

'Well, I'll have to have a word with my Eric,' Mrs Williams said. But she would say no more.

So they drove off in triumph in the silver camper; cat and kittens, James, Mandy and her grandad.

Walton quickly regained her strength in the sunny warmth of Lilac Cottage. After three more weeks Smoky, Patch, Tiddles and Eric began to bounce and tumble. They chased anything that moved. On Mr Hope's lawn they sat in wait for butterflies to land on the purple buddleia. Still as statues, they watched and waited. Then they bounced and pounced and tumbled. They always missed. They turned endless somersaults. Mandy would score them out of ten like international gymnasts doing their floor exercises.

James came often to check on Eric. He lay propped on his elbows out on the lawn, with a computer magazine spread out in front of him. He pretended to read, but really he watched

Eric's every move; his grumpy swipes with his
front paws at mischievous Smoky and Patch, his
sulking under the shade of the rhubarb leaves.

'Don't worry,' Mandy said. 'After a week in
your house he'll be as sweet-tempered and
patient as poor old Benji was. It's the Hunters'
magic way with cats!'

James looked up from his magazine
and smiled.

Mandy went down regularly to the village to
report to Ernie on Tiddles's progress. Ernie
would ask endless questions about his kitten
and waited with utter impatience for the day
when he could have her home. 'Hey!' he warned
Sammy, flipping the squirrel off his shoulder.
'Stop nipping my ear, you!' The squirrel, who

had free range of Ernie's kitchen, scampered down his back and round his waist, to cling on to his belt buckle.

Mandy laughed. 'He'll be jealous when Tiddles comes!'

'And so he should be,' Ernie said. 'I can't wait to get that kitten home!'

At Lilac Cottage, Walton fed the four kittens less and less, watched them take to solid food and grew rather bored with motherhood. These days she preferred a quiet corner in the kitchen underneath the vegetable rack, with a bit of peace and quiet. Her job was almost done.

Half-term holiday arrived. It was a green world; everyone was packing up and going home.

'Now, then,' Mr Williams grunted at Mandy by way of greeting. She was unlocking the padlock on her bike.

She glanced up. It was unusual for the caretaker to talk to her at all these days, and it was weeks since she'd seen his wife. 'Oh, great!' she muttered.

She hadn't forgiven him for hanging that dreadful threat over their heads, even though things had worked out fine in the end. The best she could do was to avoid the caretaker whenever possible. She hastily got ready to push off for home.

'How are those kittens of yours?' Mr Williams grumbled in his low, gravelly voice. 'Getting pretty big and strong by now, I should think?'

Mandy nodded.

'And I hear you've found folk willing to take them on?' he persisted. One hand was on his precious garden gate, but he looked like a man with something on his mind.

Oh, go away, just go away! Mandy thought to herself.

But instead he said, 'Come here a second,' and looked round furtively at the lace curtains of the kitchen window. 'I want to have a word!'

It involved Mandy riding back to school on the first day of her half-term holiday. She had the basket strapped carefully to the back of her bike. *Who would have believed it?* she thought to herself as she lifted the basket, reached in, and gathered Walton gently in her arms.

'Come on, Walton, come on girl!' she murmured.

'Shh!' said Mr Williams, gesturing towards

the porch. 'This is still a secret!'

Mandy nodded and set Walton down. Immaculate, ladylike, and elegant as a model on a catwalk, Walton sniffed the logs, tested the doormat, pushed the door with her paw. It swung open.

'Eric?' Mrs Williams called from inside the kitchen. Mandy grinned at the caretaker. Then, 'Eric!' Mrs Williams said again, her voice high-pitched and surprised. 'Eric, this cat has just walked back into this kitchen as if she owns the place!'

They went inside to see, and there was Mrs Williams staring down at the familiar black and white shape. 'How did she get here? Did she walk?' Mrs Williams demanded.

Her husband gave a self-conscious little laugh. 'No, as a matter of fact, Amy, I asked this young lady here to bring her back home for you!'

Mrs Williams looked up at him, her eyes filling with tears. 'Oh, Eric!'

'Aye, well!' He looked embarrassed. 'I knew you were pining for the daft cat.' He half turned towards Mandy. 'She nattered me to death about it! She's too soft by half, my wife!'

Mandy watched Walton wrap herself around

Mrs Williams's legs, purring like mad. She peered in her corner for food and looked up as if to say, 'Where is it, then?' They laughed, gave her a saucer of milk and made a great fuss of her homecoming.

'And will we take her with us?' Mrs Williams asked, still unable to believe her husband's change of heart.

'Why, where are you going?' Mandy asked.

'Eric's leaving his job.'

'He's not . . . ?' Mandy looked anxiously at the old couple. Had Mr Williams's arthritis finally beaten him?

'No, he's not got the sack,' Mrs Williams said. 'No, in fact the Headmaster only wanted to see him to ask him to stay on beyond retirement age. He said he'd never find another caretaker as good as Eric!'

Mr Williams tut-tutted.

'Yes, he did, Eric! But he came home and we talked about it, and we decided of our own accord that we'd call it a day. We're getting on a bit and we want some peace and quiet in our old age.'

Mr Williams nodded. He watched Walton grooming herself after her drink. She was sitting on the window-sill, using her front paw to clean behind her ears. 'Well!' he said, taken aback.

'I told you they're nice clean animals!' Mandy laughed.

'So we've decided to retire!' Mrs Williams announced. 'We've got our eye on one of the new bungalows just up the road!'

'A quiet little cul-de-sac, plenty of garden!' Mr Williams said.

'Perfect for Walton?' Mandy could hardly keep the smile from spreading all over her face.

The caretaker looked at his wife and broke into a grin. 'I suppose so,' he said, shaking his head.

'And will it be all right if I book Walton in at Animal Ark for her operation?' Mandy asked, trying to be tactful.

'Operation?' Mr Williams repeated slowly.

'Yes, so she won't have any more kittens.'

'Oh,' he said, very old-fashioned. '*That* operation!'

'Yes, you don't want any more little ones cluttering up your kitchen, getting in amongst your best shirts!'

Mr Williams went bright red. He looked sheepishly at his wife, then his face broke into a broad grin again. 'I should say not!' he agreed.

So Mandy made the arrangements. She wouldn't hear of them having to pay for Walton being spayed. She knew her mum and dad would want that too. So she said she would book Walton in for the following Monday. Mandy took the hand offered by Mr Williams and shook it warmly.

'No hard feelings?' he asked.

'None!' she said.

Mandy rode home along the moor road. She felt on top of the world, literally. The road crested the hill. Lapwings curved overhead in the clear sky, the moor rolled in every direction. Perfect!

She headed downhill to Welford and Animal Ark. She'd go in to see who else needed rescuing; maybe a lost hedgehog who'd found its way to the surgery, or a 'male' hamster who'd just produced six babies! ('The pet shop said it was a boy, they did really!')

The wind caught Mandy's hair. She tilted her head back and stuck her legs out sideways to freewheel down the hill. And she laughed out loud.

Kitten in the Cold

Kitten in the Cold

Special thanks to Jenny Oldfield
Thanks also to C. J. Hall, B.Vet.Med., M.R.C.V.S., for reviewing
the veterinary information contained in this book.

Animal Ark is a trademark of Working Partners Limited
Text copyright © 1996 Working Partners Limited
Created by Working Partners Limited, London WC1X 9HH
Original series created by Ben M. Baglio
Illustrations copyright © 1996 Shelagh McNicholas

First published as a single volume in Great Britain in 1996
by Hodder Children's Books

To the real Amber

One

'Mandy, are you sure you know what you're doing?' Grandad Hope asked as she lifted Smoky on to the kitchen table at Lilac Cottage.

Gran tut-tutted. 'For goodness sake, Tom, you can see that the cat is in good hands. Stop fretting and let Mandy get on with it.' She bustled to fetch a small bottle of cleanser, a bowl of hot water and some cotton wool.

'We'll need a towel,' Mandy warned. 'Smoky won't like having his ears cleaned. He'll try to shake his head. The cleanser gets everywhere.'

Grandad brought a striped red towel and

spread it on the table. 'That stuff's not too hot, is it?'

Mandy dipped the bottle into the hot water, while Smoky strolled up and down to investigate.

'Tom!' Gran said. 'Why don't you go into the lounge and read a nice gardening magazine until we've finished in here? I don't know about Mandy, but you're making me nervous!'

Mandy grinned. 'It's OK. It doesn't bother me.' Her grandad worried about two things in life; his garden and his cat. It was Grandad who'd noticed something was wrong with Smoky's ear in the first place. He told Mandy that Smoky was always scratching it and shaking his head. Mandy had gone back to Animal Ark and asked her mum and dad what it could be.

'Ear mites,' Adam Hope had suggested. 'The bites could be infected.' He'd called in at the cottage to take a look, and left Mandy there to treat poor Smoky's condition.

'Don't look!' Gran told Grandad, as Mandy settled Smoky and gently took hold of the scruff of his neck. 'Do you need any help, Mandy?'

She shook her head. 'Smoky's a good boy, aren't you? You're not going to struggle.' Speaking soothingly, Mandy very carefully put a drop or two of lukewarm liquid into the cat's ear. 'See, it's not too horrible, is it?'

Smoky opened his mouth wide and miaowed.

'There.' She massaged a spot just below his ear.

'What's that for?' Grandad ventured forward for a closer look.

'To soften the ear wax. I have to clear it out before I put some other drops in.' She worked patiently, glad that Smoky didn't fidget. Taking a piece of cotton wool, she wiped cleanser from the ear canal.

'Oops!' Grandad stood back, as suddenly Smoky shook his head. Drops splashed on to the towel.

'Nearly done,' Mandy promised. She finished off with a cotton bud, easing it down the ear to clean out the tiny, delicate folds of skin. Then Gran handed her the bottle of medicine which Adam Hope had given them. Mandy held the dropper to the infected ear and let three or four drops fall. A quick final massage and the job was done.

'Will that do the trick?' Grandad asked.

Mandy handed Smoky over to him. 'Yes. The drops will kill the mites and cure the infection.'

She'd seen it done many times at the surgery, but this was the first time she'd been trusted to do it herself. She felt pleased that it had gone well.

'Excellent!' Grandad beamed at her. 'We'll make a vet of you yet.'

'I hope so,' Mandy sighed. She longed to follow in her mum and dad's footsteps and run the surgery with them.

'Long hours, lots of stress,' Gran reminded her. She cleared the table and put on a clean cloth. 'It's not an easy job.'

But Mandy couldn't think of anything she'd rather do. She'd always loved animals. 'More than people,' her dad would joke. She spent most of her spare time lending a hand at Animal Ark with sick cats, dogs, hedgehogs; any animal that needed help. With her shoulder-length blonde hair and slight figure, Mandy could often be spotted around Welford village looking for animals in trouble.

Grandad stroked Smoky under the chin. 'You have a way with them, that's for sure. Doesn't she, Smoky?'

The young grey cat purred his agreement.

'Hardly any time off.' Gran went on putting

all the minus points about being a vet. 'Look at your mum and dad. It's coming up to Christmas, and they're busier than ever.'

Now that the kitchen table was back to normal, Mandy followed her gran into the lounge and helped her to lift a big cardboard box full of Christmas decorations down from a cupboard. She peered inside at the silver baubles and coloured lights. 'It's because of the cold,' she explained. 'Animals seem to have more accidents and illnesses this time of year.'

'Just like human beings, when you come to think about it.' Grandad put Smoky down on his favourite red cushion on the sofa and came to help. 'Coughs and colds, snuffles and sneezes.' He took a tangle of Christmas lights from the box. 'That's funny. I'm sure I put these away nice and tidy last year.'

Mandy laughed at his puzzled frown. 'Shall I untangle them for you?' She loved Christmas; putting up the decorations at Animal Ark and Lilac Cottage, making and buying presents. Smoky jumped down from the sofa and came to play. He lifted his paw to bat a light that dangled from Grandad's hand.

'Yes, please.'

So Mandy sat cross-legged on the carpet with Smoky on her lap, patiently untying the knots in the wire until the lights were straightened out, ready for use.

> *'Away in a-a manger,*
> *No-o crib for a bed,*
> *The-e little Lord Jesus*
> *La-ay down his sweet head!'*

A carol singer stood at the door.

'Dad!' Mandy recognised the voice. He sang in the church choir. 'He must be practising for a concert.'

Smoky cocked an ear, miaowed, then crept off under a chair. Gran and Grandad laughed.

> *'We three Kings of Orient are,*
> *One in a taxi, one in a car . . .'*

Gran dashed to the door to let him in before he had a chance to ruin the song any further. 'Adam, come in out of the snow!'

Mandy looked up as he stopped to take off his boots at the door. There were snowflakes in his short brown hair and melting on his beard.

He was zipped up inside his winter jacket, blowing warm air into his cold hands. 'Did you like my singing?' he said with a grin.

'Fantastic, Dad!'

'What's Smoky doing under there?' He unzipped his jacket and took it off.

'Hiding from the carol singer.'

'Hmm. He's got no ear for music, that cat.' Mandy's dad settled in a chair by the fire. 'Talking of ears, how is it?'

'Cured, we hope.' Mandy handed the lights to her grandad. 'Smoky seems to have stopped scratching already.'

'Well done. It gave me time to pop over to Bleakfell Hall. I had to check up on Pandora for Mrs Ponsonby. She's got a bit of a chill, that's all. Poor Mrs P. was worried stiff.'

'*Poor Pandora*, you mean!' Gran didn't always see eye to eye with fussy Mrs Ponsonby. 'That little Pekinese gets carried everywhere. She has no chance to run around and play like any normal dog.' She brought piping-hot tea and chocolate cake through from the kitchen. 'By the way, Adam, did you mention Father Christmas to Mrs Ponsonby?'

Mandy pricked up her ears.

He clicked his fingers. 'No, sorry. I completely forgot.'

'Brain like a sieve.' Gran tapped the top of his head. 'We need to know if she has room for Rudolph at the Hall.'

'What's this?' Mandy was full of curiosity.

Gran's eyes twinkled. 'Rudolph the red-nosed reindeer. You know the tune?'

'Da-dum, de da-da da-dum . . .' Mandy's dad came in with a deep bass version.

'Don't encourage him,' Mandy sighed. 'Yes, so what about Rudolph and Bleakfell Hall?'

'Father Christmas is going to bring his reindeer to Welford for Christmas Eve!' Gran announced. 'Of course, Rudolph will be a very tired reindeer, coming all the way from Reindeerland. So he'll need a place to stay . . .'

'Oh, Gran!' Mandy sighed. She knew better than to believe all this stuff. 'Everyone knows there's no such . . .'

'Hush. You wash your mouth out with soap and water, Mandy Hope! Father Christmas and his sleigh will be here in person, complete with reindeer. And if you don't believe me, ask **your grandad!**'

Mandy looked from one smiling face to another. 'Grandad? . . . Dad?'

They nodded back.

'What's going on?' The grown-ups were up to something. Mandy reached down to pick up Smoky, who'd come creeping close to the warm log fire. She cuddled him to her.

'Father Christmas will make a special guest appearance in the village square this year,' was all Grandad would say. 'Everyone's going to be there. Why don't you bring James along and find out?'

James Hunter, Mandy's best friend, lived on the edge of Welford. 'Will there really be a reindeer?'

'Two!' Gran said.

Mandy considered it. 'Maybe we will come and have a look.' Real reindeer with antlers, trotting through the snow! 'Wait a minute, I didn't think there were any reindeer left in this country. Didn't they all die out ages ago?'

'Aha!' Grandad winked. 'But there are plenty in Reindeerland!'

'Anyway,' Adam Hope said, 'that's where you're wrong. We do have reindeer in Britain. In Scotland, as a matter of fact. They belong to well-managed, domesticated herds in the Cairngorm Mountains. There! *Rangifer tarandus,* to give them their Latin name. They're supervised by the Reindeer Council, and looked after by a Mr Donald McNab.'

'Ask me anything you want to know about reindeer!' Grandad boasted. 'For instance, why do reindeer have cloven hooves?'

'I don't know; why *do* reindeer have cloven hooves?' Mandy joined in the fun. It really did seem as if Rudolph was coming for Christmas!

'To help them walk on frozen snow.' Grandad rushed on. 'And did you know, a reindeer can pull a sledge carrying three hundred pounds for a hundred miles a day?'

She shook her head. What was going on? How come they all knew so much about reindeer all of a sudden?

'Stop teasing,' Gran said at last, 'and tell poor Mandy why we're all reindeer-mad.'

'It's all in a good cause,' Grandad explained. 'This special guest appearance in the village is in aid of a little girl who lives at Beechtrees. That's the bungalow next to the main road. She and her family came to live in Welford earlier this year. Jeremy Hastings is the new groundsman at the tennis club. Their daughter, Alex, is only five, but they've recently found out that she's seriously ill.'

Mandy tried to connect the reindeer's visit with Alex Hastings. She'd seen the girl from a distance; a tiny, red-haired child, with a bigger brother. Their hair was the first thing you noticed about them both. It was curly and shone reddish-gold in the sun. 'What's wrong with her?'

'Something to do with her heart. She needs an operation, Mandy dear.' Gran spoke softly, seriously. 'There's only one place in the world where she can get this kind of operation, and that's in America. But the Hastings can't afford to take her there. Your grandad got to hear about it one day at the tennis club. A few people put their heads together and came up with various ways of raising money so the family could go to the States.

'Fund-raising,' Mandy's dad chipped in. 'Everyone has been having bright ideas. Your grandad came up with this special invitation to Father Christmas and his reindeer. We hope the whole of Welford will come along, sing a few carols and put lots of money in a collection-box.'

'People have been very good so far,' Grandad said. 'We've already raised enough money for the operation, but we need another eight hundred pounds for the air fares to send Alex and her family for treatment. And we need it quickly. She must go early in the New Year for the operation, otherwise it'll be too late.'

'You mean, if she doesn't get it, she'll die?' Mandy whispered.

'I'm afraid so, love.'

For a while, everyone was silent. The logs crackled in the hearth, Smoky rubbed his soft face against Mandy's cheek.

'But if she goes to America and has the operation, the doctors think she will be completely cured,' Gran said. 'So you see, Father Christmas's visit is going to be extra-important this year.'

Slowly Mandy said. 'Does Alex know about going to America?'

Gran shook her head. 'Her mum and dad think it's best to keep quiet until they're sure they can take her. She doesn't really know how ill she is. And she certainly doesn't have a clue about Father Christmas's visit!'

Adam Hope finished his cup of tea and

brushed cake crumbs from his sweater. Smoky jumped from Mandy's arms and went to see whether the crumbs were worth eating. 'I saw Alex's dad today, as a matter of fact.'

'At Animal Ark?' Mandy found the little girl's story sad but fascinating.

'Yes. He brought a kitten in for her vaccinations. They've only just got her. Alex loves animals, apparently. Her dad says the walls of her bedroom are plastered with pictures of them!' He glanced at Mandy with a little smile.

'Just like someone else we know!' Grandad teased. Mandy's own room was a portrait gallery of pets, wild animals and endangered species.

'Beechtrees is just past Susan Collins's house, isn't it?' Mandy ignored them and got to thinking ahead instead.

'That's right. Why?' Her grandad bent to plug in the Christmas lights. They lit up, a brilliant chain of blue, green and pink. 'Hey presto!'

'Oh, nothing . . .' A five-year-old girl with a new kitten! 'What's the kitten like?' she asked her dad, as casually as possible.

'She's a little brown and black tortoiseshell.'

'Sweet!' Mandy stared wistfully at Smoky, now

a fully-grown cat. 'How old?'

'Four or five months, just at the playful stage. You know, she chases everything, including her own tail.'

'Aah!'

'And she has the most amazing eyes,' her dad continued. 'Big and shiny in her cute little dark face.'

'What colour?' She wanted to picture the kitten perfectly.

'Her eyes? They're a sort of bright gold colour. Traffic-light orange. Yes, that's it!' Mr Hope smiled as he stood up, ready to take Mandy home. He stroked Smoky. 'Not as good-looking as you, of course,' he said with a grin. 'But the Hastings' kitten does have the most amazing amber eyes. And that's what they've called her. Alex chose the name herself; Amber.'

They put on their jackets and boots, said goodbye to Mandy's grandparents and Smoky, and began to tramp through the snow up the lane to Animal Ark, Mr Hope whistling as they walked.

'Dad?'

'What?' He stopped mid-tune.

'I wonder if I should go and visit Alex and

Amber,' Mandy said dreamily. There was a white wonderland of snow-laden trees, drifts almost a metre deep against the walls, stars in a moonlit sky.

'I don't see why not.'

'And, Dad...'

'Uh-oh!' He gathered snow from the wall-top and patted it into shape. His eyes gleamed as he aimed the ball at Mandy. 'Come on, this is a challenge!'

'No, Dad, I want to ask you something!' But she couldn't resist scooping up snow and making her own snowball.

'So I gather. Am I going to say yes? I know you when you give me that look!' He was laughing now, as the first snowball flew towards him. He dodged just in time.

'Listen!' Mandy dived for more ammunition. 'You know Gran thought that the two reindeer might be able to stay at Bleakfell Hall?'

It was her dad's turn to fling a snowball. It thudded against Mandy's shoulder. 'Direct hit! Yes, Mrs Ponsonby has an empty stable at the back of the Hall.'

'Well, we could look after them at Animal Ark instead, couldn't we? We've got room in the

residential unit. I mean, reindeer aren't all that big!' She stood with her arm raised, fresh snow poised ready.

'Gi-normous!' Mr Hope dodged and slipped. He landed flat on his back.

Mandy ran over and stood, hands on hips, 'But Mrs Ponsonby wouldn't have a clue how to look after them. We would! You and mum must know all about reindeer.'

'Flattery will get you . . . everywhere!' He grinned back up at her.

'You mean yes? The reindeer can stay with us?' She hauled him to his feet.

'For a couple of nights. As long as your mum agrees.'

'Yippee!' Mandy charged into a drift and kicked up loose snow. It sprayed up and sparkled. 'Oh, Dad, thanks! Oh, brilliant!' She ran ahead up the lane to Animal Ark. Real reindeer were coming to stay!

Two

'Two reindeer?' Emily Hope was talking on the phone in Reception. Jean Knox, Animal Ark's receptionist, stood listening, her glasses perched high on her forehead. Simon, their nurse, came through from a treatment room, ready for morning surgery. He raised his eyebrows at Mandy when he overheard the conversation.

It was early the next morning; only three days to go until Christmas Eve, and Mandy was keeping her fingers firmly crossed. Her mum had just rung the owner of the reindeer herd in Scotland to make arrangements for the visit.

'Rudolph and Dasher?' Mrs Hope smiled.

'And you'll bring their food with them?'

Mandy's eyes shone. 'We're having two reindeer to stay this Christmas!' she whispered to Simon.

'You must be joking!' Glancing up from the appointment book, he realised that Mandy was serious. 'When?'

'Tomorrow, Wednesday.'

'How will they travel? By flying across the rooftops?' Simon winked at Jean, who seemed to think that the entire Hope family had finally gone crazy.

'I don't know yet. Hang on a minute.' Mandy listened in again.

'We have an open-air compound at the back of Animal Ark, where we exercise the patients. It's small, but secure. I think that should be all right. You say the reindeer need to stay out overnight . . . Yes, OK. Someone could meet you in Walton and show you the road over the moor to Welford. It's hard to find if you don't know your way around . . . We've had snow, but the main roads are fairly clear. Yes, fine.'

They waited as arrangements went ahead.

'Tomorrow afternoon? Yes, one of us will be

there. We'll meet you outside the bus station in town . . . you should be able to park a trailer there . . . Just look out for our Animal Ark Land-rover . . . yes, bye, Mr McNab!' Emily Hope nodded as she put down the phone.

'Correct me if I'm wrong, but did I just hear you break your strictest Animal Ark rule?' Jean asked in disbelief. She'd known the Hopes a long time, and never in living memory had Mandy's mum and dad agreed to let an animal who didn't need treatment come to stay.

'You did.' Mrs Hope put on her white coat.

'Here comes our first patient.' Mandy hopped off her stool and went to the window. She wanted to change the subject. A car struggled down the lane through the snow. It looked like the Parker Smythes' big four-wheel drive.

'Well, I never!' Jean still couldn't believe it.

'They're coming down from a place near Aviemore,' Mrs Hope said. 'It's quite a journey. Donald McNab is driving down in a trailer . . . to help Father Christmas deliver presents in Welford!'

'Mum!' It looked as if Mandy would have to go along with the Father Christmas thing, though she considered herself much too old.

'What's wrong? You still hang up your stocking for him, don't you?'

'Yes, but . . . oh, OK, you win!' Mandy beamed.

'It's all in a good cause.' Her mum explained to Jean the idea behind the reindeer's visit. 'We're trying to raise money to send little Alex Hastings to America. You know about her operation, don't you?' Soon everyone in Welford would be in on it, thought Mandy.

'Good idea. I'll be there,' Jean promised. 'After all, it is Christmas.'

'Seven-thirty in the square on Christmas Eve?' Simon asked. 'Count me in too.' Mrs Parker Smythe and her eight-year-old daughter, Imogen, had just brought their pet rabbits, Button and Barney, into the surgery. He showed them into a treatment room. 'Did you hear about Father Christmas's special visit?' he asked them, as the door swung to.

'The more the merrier,' Emily Hope smiled. She turned to Mandy. 'Happy now?'

'I can't wait!'

'Well, why not go and visit Alex, like you planned? I'm sure she could do with some company.'

'Now?' Mandy would normally help out in the

surgery during the school holidays.

'Why not? We won't be busy here, not in this weather. And you could tell her there's a special treat in store this Christmas.'

'But not exactly what the treat is?' Mandy scrambled out of her white coat and grabbed her jacket.

Mrs Hope put her head to one side, ready to start work. 'No,' she said. 'Let's keep Father Christmas as a nice surprise!'

'Alex likes animals,' Mandy promised James. She'd called at the Hunter's house, and James had decided to bring his dog, Blackie, along to Beechtrees.

The black Labrador padded through the snow ahead of them, leaving a narrow trail of footprints. When he came to the wide gates of Susan Collins's grand house, he stopped.

'No, Blackie, that's not where we're going today,' James ordered him on. James was dressed for the snow in a padded jacket and a baseball cap worn back-to-front. The wind had reddened his cheeks, and his glasses reflected the bright light as he and Mandy loped along after Blackie.

Beechtrees was tucked away under the shadow

of some tall trees a few hundred metres along the main road from Susan's house. Today there were few cars on the road; only a yellow snow-remover trundling towards them, with Jeremy Hastings sitting at the controls. The plough had been clearing a track from the tennis club towards the main road after the snowfall of the previous night.

'Hello there.' Mr Hastings drew near, then leaned sideways. He was puzzled by the sight of Blackie, James and Mandy knee-deep in the fresh snow.

'Hello.' Mandy knew him as friendly in a quiet sort of way, never excited or annoyed. She and James had seen him at work around the tennis courts that autumn.

Blackie spoiled the introductions by barking at the snow-plough.

'Sorry.' James blushed and told him to sit. 'He's never seen one close up before.'

'That's OK.' Jeremy Hastings decided to take a break. He climbed down from the cab. 'I know you two, don't I?'

'Yes. I'm James Hunter, and this is Blackie.'

'And I'm Mandy Hope.' Somehow, because Mr Hastings was shy, Mandy was self-conscious too. She felt her face grow hot behind her woollen scarf and hat.

'The vets' daughter?'

She nodded.

'I took Alex's kitten up to Animal Ark for her yesterday. Nice place.' He didn't waste words. 'Alex doesn't get out much at the moment.'

'No. That's why we've brought Blackie to see her,' James said.

Mandy's blonde hair fell around her face as she took off her hat. 'We heard she likes animals.'

'She's mad about them!' For the first time, Jeremy Hastings smiled. 'Completely cuckoo. She'll love you, Blackie. Why don't you all come in?'

Mandy felt that the ice was broken. She grinned at James and followed the groundsman between two tall beech trees, up a path towards the bungalow.

'Alex!' Mr Hastings opened the door and knocked snow off his boots. 'You've got visitors!'

They waited for an answer, but none came.

'She's a bit shy with strangers,' her father told them. 'Hang on a sec.' He kicked off his wellingtons and went inside.

'Sit, Blackie.' James made him wait inside the porch. He and Mandy stared curiously into the hallway.

'What do you want?' a voice challenged from behind them.

They spun round. Blackie jumped up. There in the front garden, peering from behind a bush, was a small boy with bright ginger hair. His eyes were greeny-grey, his face covered in freckles. He wore a navy-blue fleece jacket zipped to his chin, and an expression that said 'Get lost!'

'We've come to play with Alex,' Mandy answered carefully. The boy looked about seven years old.

'Oh, her.' He turned away in disgust. 'She doesn't want to play.' He trudged back on to the lawn and kicked at the deep snow. 'I'm her brother, and she won't even play with me.'

Mandy couldn't tell who the boy was most angry with, but his tone of voice and his deep frown made her guess that it was everyone and everything. He was what Gran would call 'mardy'. This meant he sulked a lot.

'I'll play with you,' James volunteered. It was chilly standing on the porch waiting for Alex to appear. 'We could build a snowman.'

'Where?'

'There on the lawn.'

'How tall?'

'As tall as you like.'

'Up to the roof of the bungalow?' The boy looked up at the single storey house.

'Well, maybe not that tall.' James went ahead anyway. He jumped from the step into the garden and began to scoop snow into a rough pile. 'Let's see how fat we can make him.'

Mandy pulled her hat from her pocket. 'He can wear this when you've finished him.'

Slowly the boy came and took it. 'Can he wear your scarf too?'

'OK.' She unwound it and handed it over.

Satisfied, he ran back to James. Soon they were both hard at work on the snowman's body.

'There, what did I tell you?' Mr Hastings returned at last, holding his daughter's hand. 'Here's a dog come all this way in the snow to see you. He's called Blackie.'

Blackie stood up and wagged his tail at the sound of his name.

Mandy knelt and put an arm around his neck. 'He won't bite,' she said softly. 'He's a nice doggie.'

Alex Hastings let go of her father's hand and took a halting step forward. She was small for a five-year-old; pale and thin, wearing a dark blue corduroy dress. Her curly hair was even brighter than Mandy's mum's; the reddest hair that she had ever seen.

Alex's big green eyes grew wide as she reached out a tiny hand to stroke Blackie. 'He's all wet!' She took it quickly away.

'That's melted snow. Blackie likes the snow. He tries to eat it!'

Alex stroked him again. 'His ears are nice and soft.'

'He's one big softie really.' Mandy smiled as the little girl grew bolder. 'Would your new kitten like to meet him?'

Alex looked up at her dad. 'Won't the dog chase Amber?'

'I don't think so. Blackie's probably used to cats. Why not fetch Amber from your bedroom and see?'

As Alex went slowly through one of the doors leading off from the square hallway, Mr Hastings smiled at Mandy. 'Bring Blackie inside and let me close the door. Alex's mum is fixing hot chocolate for everyone. We can all do with it on a day like today.'

Mandy smiled back, stepped in and looked round at the cream coloured walls, the big mirror and framed family photographs.

'Dad, Amber won't come!' Alex called in a high, panicky voice. 'She's hiding under the bed.'

There was a faint miaow. Blackie pricked up his ears and whined.

'No, she's not! She's running away!'

They heard rapid little feet pattering and jumping from surface to surface, then a small black and brown shape hurtled through the door. The kitten somersaulted into the hall.

'Oh, Amber!' Alex cried from her bedroom.

'It's OK, here she is!' Mr Hastings cornered the kitten and picked her up.

Mandy held on to Blackie as Alex came slowly over and took Amber from her father. All Mandy could see was a bundle of wriggling fur, a long, fluffy tail and a little pair of pointed ears. 'She's gorgeous!' she exclaimed.

'Amber, be good,' Alex scolded. 'Say hello to Blackie.'

But the kitten caught sigh of the big black dog and stared. Her golden eyes flashed, and she opened her mouth wide and hissed.

'No, you have to be nice to him,' Alex insisted. She brought her up closer. 'Nice doggie. See, Amber; nice, nice doggie!'

Good-natured Blackie sniffed at the kitten. Amber's ears and whiskers twitched. She put out a paw to pat the dog's black nose.

'See, you like him!' Soon it was safe to let go of the kitten. Alex put her on the carpet and watched the two animals stalk in circles around each other. Blackie towered over the kitten, but he was very gentle. Amber, on the other hand, thought that playing meant jumping up at

Blackie and catching hold of his neck. She clung on for dear life.

Alex gasped, then laughed. 'They're having a game!'

Mandy told her all about Blackie and James. 'James is my best friend. He helps us with the animals at Animal Ark.' She explained that her mum and dad looked after sick animals.

Alex didn't take her eyes off Amber and Blackie. 'Are they all sick?' she asked slowly.

'Who, the patients who come to my house?' Mandy nodded. 'But most of them get better. It's like a hospital for animals.'

The little girl turned to her with a serious face. 'I've been to hospital.'

'I know,' Mandy said gently.

'I might have to go again, so they can make me better. Then I can play out with William.'

'That's her brother,' Mr Hastings explained.

'I know. We met him in the garden. James is out there building a snowman with him.' Mandy took Alex to the glass door to look outside. The snowman was already as high as William's shoulder.

'Who's building a snowman?' Alex's mother, popped her head around the kitchen door.

'William and James.' Alex peered out wistfully at the snowy scene. Then she turned her attention back to the two animals. 'Amber's got a friend,' she told her mum.

Mrs Hastings stepped into view. She was small and neat, in dark trousers and a soft, fawn-coloured jumper. Her short hair was a darker red than her children's, with rich coppery tints.

She smiled at Mandy. 'So have you,' she said to her daughter. 'A new friend. What a lovely surprise!'

Mandy was soon made to feel welcome in the Hastings' house. Alex took her and Blackie into her bedroom. From there they could see James and William out in the garden. The snowman was growing; he had a head and a face made from twigs and stones.

'What's Father Christmas bringing you?' Alex sat on her bed with Amber on her lap. Surrounded by pillows and cushions, she looked like a little red-haired doll.

'I'm not sure.' Mandy smiled.

'Do you believe in him?' Alex asked solemnly. She didn't give Mandy a chance to reply. 'I do! I wrote to him with a list of things.'

'What did you ask for?'

'Well, it's not things exactly. Anyway, I can't tell. It's a secret. Otherwise it won't come true, like a wish.'

Beneath the bright chatter, Mandy suspected that Alex was sad. From the way she sat stroking her kitten, she could even imagine what Alex's wish might have been. 'Dear Father Christmas, Please give me an operation to make me better, so I can go out and play.'

'Do you like reindeers?' Alex chatted on. 'I do! My favourite is Rudolph. Who's your favourite?'

Mandy glanced up at the giant colour pictures of kittens and puppies, ponies and hamsters. She could hardly see a square centimetre of bare wall space. 'Rudolph.' She bit her lip. Sometimes it was difficult not to spill the beans. Little did Alex know it, but she was about to get a visit from her favourite reindeer!

'Poor Rudolph, he couldn't join in any reindeer games, could he?' Alex sighed.

'Because his nose was too red. They didn't like him,' Mandy reminded her.

'I would have let him join in anyway.'

'Me too.' Mandy sat on the floor with Blackie,

happy to talk to Alex as if Rudolph was a real, live reindeer. Alex seemed to know the story inside out.

'What did it matter what colour his nose was?' Alex was determined to stick up for Santa's problem helper. 'When I'm better, anyone who wants to can play with me! I'll go back to school, and *everyone* can be my friend!'

Mandy agreed. Suddenly, there was a loud thud against the window. They turned quickly, in time to see a flattened snowball sliding down the glass.

'William!' Alex gasped. The windowpane had rattled. Startled, Amber had jumped from her lap and gone into hiding. Blackie gave a sharp bark.

'Alex, come and look!' The boy's voice from the garden was high and bossy. Another snowball landed against the glass.

Slowly Alex uncrossed her legs. Mandy helped her from the bed. She could only move at a snail's pace, Mandy realised, and was quickly out of breath.

'Come here. Look at this!'

From the window, the girls could see two snowmen. One wore Mandy's red and white striped hat and scarf. The other had James's cap perched on his head.

'What's going on in here?' Mrs Hastings came rushing into the room with a worried frown. She glanced at the melting snowballs sliding slowly down the windowpane. 'What was that noise?'

'William's snowballs. Look what they've built in the garden!' Alex's face was bright with admiration.

But Mrs Hastings was annoyed as she came to the window.

From outside, William saw his mother and yelled. 'Mum, look!' He sounded faint through the glass, but they could tell he was proud of the snowmen. 'Can Alex come out and see?'

Mrs Hastings tapped hard on the window. 'No, she can't!' she mouthed. 'And you come inside at once!'

Mandy saw the smile vanish from William's face. James stood by, unsure.

'Alex, it's time for your medicine,' her mother said sharply. Frowning, she left the room to fetch it.

'William's for it now,' Alex whispered. 'He's not supposed to do things that make me jump.'

She sighed and retreated to her bed. 'Now he'll think it's my fault that he's in trouble again.'

'Oh, I'm sure he won't,' Mandy began. But she heard doors bang and Mrs Hastings' voice going on at her son.

'. . . No consideration . . . making loud noises . . . you're seven years old; old enough to know better, William!'

Alex hung her head and put her hands over her ears.

'We'd better be off,' Mandy said quickly. James still stood out there in the cold.

Alex nodded. 'I have to have a nap after my medicine anyway.' She blushed and smiled. 'Thanks for bringing Blackie to see me.'

'Thanks for showing me Amber.' The kitten peeped out from under the bed, her eyes shining big and golden. 'Enjoy the snowmen!' Alex would be able to see them from her bed. Mandy smiled again and left.

Outside, she found James waiting for her, and, at the gate, the worried figure of Jeremy Hastings.

'Alex has to be kept nice and quiet, see,' he said to explain Mrs Hastings' anger about the snowballs. 'No exertion. It's doctors' orders. Of course, if she gets her operation, it'll be a different story. She'll be running round just like she was before.'

'Grandad says the fund-raising is going really well,' Mandy said.

He nodded and smiled grimly. 'A lot depends on this Father Christmas thing.'

'Don't worry. It'll be amazing; a sleigh, a real reindeer – Alex will love it!'

'You didn't mention it to her?'

'No.' It had been hard, but Mandy had kept the secret.

'Good. It's bound to cheer her up, isn't it?' Mr Hastings gazed up at the trees, as if he would find an answer there to his family's problems. 'Alex has always loved Father Christmas and his reindeer.'

Mandy and James said goodbye. They left Mr Hastings standing by his snow-plough, gazing up at the grey sky.

Three

'I'm sorry I'm late.' Donald McNab strolled up to the Animal Ark Land-rover.

It was just before tea next day, and Mandy and James had driven into Walton with Mr Hope to meet their special guests. After an hour of sitting freezing in the car, with James snuffling and sneezing into his hankie, Mandy's dad had nipped off to buy warm drinks. It had been a long, cold wait.

'Aye, I lost my way,' the Scotsman explained in a heavy accent. He sounded very calm. 'Took a couple of wrong turnings in York. Terrible place to drive through. I went around the old

city walls three times before I found the right
exit. My head was spinning by the time I
got out.'

'That's OK.' Mandy and James looked eagerly
for the reindeer in Mr McNab's trailer, which
he'd parked a few metres up the road. They
weren't interested in why he was late.

'I thought maybe I'd missed you.' He shook
hands as first James, then Mandy jumped down
on to the pavement. His grey eyes shone with
good humour, his handshake was firm. 'It was
good of you to wait.'

'Dad won't be long,' Mandy said. 'Mr McNab,
can we go and take a peep?' All day she'd been
looking forward to this.

'At Rudolph and Dasher? Aye, go right ahead.
And call me Don!' He fished deep in the pocket
of his weatherproof jacket. 'Here, you can give
them a wee treat for being cooped up in that
trailer for so long.'

They took a handful each of what looked
suspiciously like scraps of chewed leather. James
sniffed them and wrinkled his nose.

'Dried mushrooms,' Don laughed. 'They
love 'em!'

Mandy couldn't wait a moment longer. She

ran ahead. From inside the grey trailer came a loud shuffling and knocking of hooves. She saw that the back doors were half open, like stable doors, and as she drew near, two heads loomed out; two long noses, two pairs of dark brown eyes, and two sets of enormous antlers.

Mandy held her breath. The animals were only the height of a small Welsh pony, but their antlers were huge, branching off like mighty boughs on a tree. They curved over the reindeer's heads as they nodded and poked them out of the trailer.

'Go ahead!' Don encouraged. 'They won't harm you!'

Gingerly Mandy reached up with the mushrooms. The nearest reindeer bent to nibble at them with his velvety mouth.

'That's Dasher.'

James followed suit, letting the other reindeer nip food from his palm.

'And that's Rudolph. Say hello, boys!'

The reindeer snorted and grunted. The trailer shook as they shifted their weight.

By now a small crowd had gathered. Walton had never seen a reindeer in the flesh. Word went round for people to come and look at their

magnificent antlers. Mothers came with children, shopkeepers stood out on the pavement. One bus-driver even stopped his bus to let his passengers see, while Don McNab fielded eager questions.

'They've come to help Father Christmas,' he explained to the smallest children. 'They have to pull his sleigh through the snow.'

'When?'

'Where?'

'Will we see them?' More questions, more round eyes and open mouths.

'Aye, you will if you come to Welford on Christmas Eve,' Don told them. 'That's when the old gentleman will bring your presents!' He winked at James and Mandy.

Through all the fuss, Rudolph and Dasher chewed contentedly, until Adam Hope came back with the drinks and the children had to say goodbye.

'Do you think you'll be able to follow us OK?' Mandy's dad asked Don, after the two men had met.

But Mandy came up with a better idea. She arranged to drive with Don in the reindeer van. 'Just in case they can't keep up,' she explained.

'Och aye, I don't want to get lost again!' Don helped her into the passenger seat. All the way home, out of town and across the moor, Mandy was able to fire questions at him.

'What do reindeer eat?' she asked, hoping she'd be able to help feed them later.

'Grass, moss, ferns, bark, oh aye and mushrooms, of course.' Don answered, as he drove carefully down the hill towards Welford. The whole valley lay under a blanket of snow, and the village lights twinkled in the dusk. He stifled a yawn. 'I'm away to my bed early tonight.'

Mandy smiled happily. 'We'll take care of the reindeer for you,' she promised.

'Aye, I know you will. Anyhow, I've a busy day tomorrow.'

It would be Thursday tomorrow, the day before Christmas Eve. 'Where do you have to go?' Mandy asked.

'I've to drive the reindeer to a children's hospital in Leeds tomorrow morning. The old gentleman will be handing out presents there.'

Mandy shot a puzzled look at the cheerful little Scotsman. He had short grey hair, a square face, a nice, outdoorsy feel. 'This old gentleman . . .' she began.

'Father Christmas, aye?'

'I mean, aren't you . . . Isn't it really? . . .' She stammered to a halt. Here was another grown-up who liked to tease.

'Me?' He roared with laughter and thumped the steering wheel. 'Oh no, dearie! Don't ever let him catch you saying such a thing, or there'll be no presents for you this year!'

He went on chuckling as they followed Mr Hope and James through the village, past the pub and the post office, along the lane to Animal Ark.

Four

'Hold him steady,' Don told Mandy as she led Rudolph down the ramp from the trailer into the yard.

The reindeer tossed his head and pawed the ground stiffly until he grew used to his new surroundings.

'Here come the guests of honour.' Emily Hope stood on the step after evening surgery.

'They're . . . awesome!' Simon gave a low whistle. 'Look at those antlers!'

Rudolph grunted suspiciously, then allowed Mandy to lead him on. She took him round the back to the residential area and gave him a reward. 'Good boy.' She stroked his thick white winter mane.

'Steady as you go.' Don steered James and Dasher down the ramp. He took a look at the high wire fence surrounding the exercise compound. 'Aye, this'll do nicely.'

Mandy breathed a sigh of relief. The reindeer's long journey had ended safely. 'Will they need food?' she asked Don, anxious again as Rudolph and Dasher began to paw at the snow. 'They must be hungry.'

'No need. They can dig, see.'

The reindeer lowered their heads and began to scrape with their antlers, using them as giant snow-shovels. Soon they were down to green grass and grazing happily.

Mandy, James, Adam and Emily Hope, Simon and Jean all gathered round to watch. 'They don't seem to mind an audience,' Mr Hope said quietly.

'Och, they're used to it. They're at the centre of the action wherever they go.' Don went to fetch his own bag from the battered white van. He looked up at the soft snowflakes floating out of the dark sky. 'Good reindeer weather. It reminds them of home.'

'Come inside and get warm.' Unless there was an emergency call during the evening, Emily Hope had finished work for the day. She took Don's bag and carried it into the house. Simon and Jean went inside to tidy up the surgery.

'Aye, in a wee while.' Don grinned at Mandy and James. 'I just want to show these two the sleigh belonging to the old gentleman himself!' He stayed out in the yard as the other grown-ups went indoors.

James and Mandy shrugged and followed.

'But it's the trailer!' James was disappointed. Father Christmas's sleigh was just like any other trailer that you would see on a farm, or at a horse show.

'Not just any ordinary trailer, young Jim!' Don McNab leaped into action. He unscrewed nuts and bolts, removed the detachable roof, folded down fibreglass flaps, and soon transformed the trailer into what looked for all the world like an old-fashioned sleigh.

'Wow!' James was impressed. The painted side panels hid the wheels and looked like imitation sledge runners.

'Abracadabra! We hitch the reindeer on to

the front, and jingle bells, off we go!'

'That's really neat,' Mandy said.

'Aye, it is.'

'Who thought of it?' James tipped his glasses more firmly on to his nose and went to inspect it more closely.

'I did.' Don was proud of his handiwork. 'I use it to tour the country at Christmas time. In two shakes I can turn the trailer into the old gentleman's sleigh. He arrives in style to visit the kiddies in hospital, or turn on the Christmas lights, whatever they want.'

'I like it!' James examined the hinges and moulded fibreglass, and the metal shafts which harnessed the reindeer.

'Then why not come with us tomorrow?' Don promptly invited them both along. 'We're off to visit the wee kids in hospital in Leeds. You two can keep me on the right road.' He reminded them how hopeless he was at finding his way.

'Great; we could help look after Rudolph and Dasher!' Mandy jumped at the chance. She ran inside to ask her mum and dad.

'Yes, fine,' Emily Hope said. She stood by the stove in the warm kitchen. 'Would you tell Don that supper's ready?'

They sat down to steaming plates of thick soup and piles of fresh bread. Don McNab ate with a ravenous appetite, entertaining them with stories of the reindeer herd at home. Mandy lapped it all up; the rolling sound of the Scotsman's voice, the picture he painted of snowy mountains and magnificent animals.

Before she went to bed, Mandy went outside to check one last time on Rudolph and Dasher. They were still happily shovelling snow with their antlers to reach the grass. Tomorrow, Mandy and James would go with them to visit the children in hospital. The day after would be Grandad's fund-raising event for Alex. Mandy sighed and let the light snowflakes settle on her nose. This was going to be the most exciting Christmas ever!

'Two days to go before I open my stocking!' Simon rubbed his hands as he came in next morning. He was wearing layers of jumpers under his jacket, and a woolly hat was pulled down over his forehead. Outside, it was sunny but freezing cold.

Mandy had been up bright and early, along with her parents, while their Scots guest slept in. She'd already answered the phone to half a dozen worried pet owners. The appointment book was full.

'Just think, back home for Christmas Day; a lie-in, presents, turkey and Christmas pud!' Simon put on his white coat.

'Can we fit Mr Pickard in?' Mandy ran her finger down the list of appointments. Walter was on the phone to say that his old cat, Tom, was off-colour.

Simon nodded. 'We'll squeeze him in, but don't tell Jean.'

So Mandy made the appointment. 'He'd like to come in straight away. He sounds worried.'

And that was the start of a pre-Christmas rush at Animal Ark. At half-past eight, Jean arrived and took over from Mandy at the desk. Mandy put on her white coat, ready to help her mum and dad. There were three dogs, two cats, a hamster and a hedgehog to feed and clean.

And of course, there were Rudolph and Dasher to see to. As she went out with a special mix of oats and molasses recommended by Don, the reindeer raised their heads in greeting. Dasher trotted straight up to his dish of cereal and tucked in, but Rudolph took one sniff at his and turned up his nose. *That's strange*, Mandy thought. She patted his shaggy neck, frowned and went back inside.

Then there was a waiting-room full of patients, with old Walter Pickard and Tom at the front of the queue. Mandy was on hand as they came into Mr Hope's treatment room.

'Let's take a look at this old chap.' Mandy's dad waited for Walter to lift Tom out of his basket.

Tom appeared, sad and bedraggled. Normally a sturdy, heavyweight cat, black and white, barrel-shaped, with a black patch of fur over one eye, today he looked thin and ill. He snuffled, his head hung low, his eyes dull.

Adam Hope examined his eyes and throat. 'Has he been eating properly?'

Walter shook his head. 'He's gone right off his grub. It's not like Tom.'

'Has he been sneezing? Coughing?' Mr Hope beckoned Mandy to take a look. 'See these little ulcers on his tongue?'

She nodded. 'Is it cat flu?'

'It looks like it.' He took Tom's temperature and confirmed that it was high.

Walter sighed. The old man treated Tom as a companion. Like him, the cat was a tough customer, but getting on in years. And this year, Walter had forgotten to have him vaccinated. 'Can you do anything for him?'

Mr Hope stroked Tom. 'He'll need antibiotics to treat any secondary infection, and plenty of fluid, but you should be able to take him home and nurse him there. You'll have to keep him warm. Clean up his eyes and nostrils if they get blocked. Poor old chap, he's having trouble breathing.'

'He's feeling sorry for himself all right.'

Mr Hope decided to dose Tom with antibiotics there and then. Mandy helped to hold the cat, as her father showed Walter the best way to get the syrup down his throat. 'Remember, this is a virus infection,' he explained. 'You'll have to wash Tom's bedding and feeding bowls, then disinfect them. Don't let him near other cats, OK?'

Walter promised to take good care of him. 'Thank you, Mr Hope,' he said meekly, as he put Tom back in his basket.

'Give us a ring to let us know how you're getting along with the medicine. And don't worry, we'll soon have him back on his feet, terrorising the neighbourhood again!'

The old man smiled weakly. 'I hope you're right.' He shuffled out of the room with his pet.

Mr Hope glanced at Mandy. 'And don't you worry! Tom will be fine.'

'It's not that.' Mandy frowned. 'It's Rudolph.' She remembered that he too had sounded chesty when she took out the dish of food. And he had the look that Tom had come in with; dull-eyed and moping. She told her dad how the reindeer had turned down the oats.

'Hmm. Do you want me to take a look?'

Though the waiting-room was full to overflowing, Mandy nodded.

'Come on then, quick!'

They went out together into the snowy compound, where the difference between the two reindeer was now quite clear. Dasher, whom Mandy recognised by his shorter antlers and dark coat, came trotting nimbly, hooves clicking. But Rudolph kept his distance and gazed listlessly. When Mandy and Adam Hope approached him, he simply lowered his head

and sat down in the snow.

'Not so good.' Adam Hope frowned. 'It looks like you were right, Mandy. We may have a sick reindeer on our hands.'

They examined Rudolph and brought Don out to look. Mr Hope diagnosed a viral infection which needed the kind of treatment he'd prescribed for Tom. 'Plenty of food, plenty of water. Keep him separate from Dasher.'

Don nodded. He had talked Rudolph back on to his feet and stood patting his neck.

'He should be over it in a day or two. Perhaps

even in time for Christmas. It's a kind of twenty-four hour reindeer flu.'

But this left Don with a problem. 'I can't let the kiddies down this morning,' he told them.

'Can Dasher pull the sleigh by himself?' Mandy asked.

'He can just about manage it if Father Christmas walks alongside instead of sitting on top. You think I should go ahead and leave Rudolph behind to recover?'

'I'll stay here to look after him!' Mandy promised.

So when James arrived, full of cold but ready for the trip into Leeds, he and Don led Dasher into the trailer and prepared to set off alone.

'You're sure you don't mind, Mandy?' James asked.

'No. We're really busy in the surgery in any case. I'll be more use staying here.'

'Aye, you look after Rudolph.' Don sat at the wheel, ready to move off.

'. . . the red-nosed reindeer!' James grinned.

'Ha-ha!' She grinned back. 'Don't get lost!' she called, as the van and trailer eased out of the yard.

'Very funny!' James leaned out and waved a

map. 'Don't worry, we'll be back by teatime!'

'Mandy!' Jean called her inside. 'Would you mind manning the telephone for the next hour? Surgery is overrunning, and I did promise that I'd nip into the village to meet Lydia Fawcett for coffee. I tried to ring High Cross to cancel it, but she'd already left.'

Mandy agreed willingly. She took over in Reception, seeing the last patients into the treatment rooms and answering the busy phone. Every now and then she would glance out at Rudolph. He seemed the same; no better, no worse.

'Welford 703267, Animal Ark!' She picked up the phone. It was nearly lunchtime. Her dad had gone out on an emergency call to Sam Western's dairy herd at Upper Welford Hall. Her mum was busy treating patients in the unit.

'Hello?' A woman's voice hesitated. 'This may not be the right thing to do, but I wondered if you could give me some advice?'

'Mrs Hastings?' Mandy recognised the voice. 'Is it something to do with Amber?' Her first thought was that the kitten might have developed a case of cat flu, like Walter's Tom.

'Oh, hello, Mandy. Actually it is. It's OK, she's

not ill. It's nothing like that.'

Mandy was relieved but puzzled.

'It's a silly thing in a way . . .'

'Shall I fetch Mum?'

'No, I really don't want to bother her. Perhaps you could help. You see, Amber's been rather naughty this morning. She was in a mischievous mood, playing hide-and-seek. Anyway, Alex lost her. We looked, but we couldn't find her anywhere inside the house. But when my husband came home for lunch a few minutes ago, he spotted where Amber was.' Mrs Hastings paused for breath.

'Where?' Mandy pictured the garden path, the porch, the single storey building.

'On the roof! I went out to look, and there she was, the naughty little thing, perched halfway up, refusing to come down!'

'Do you think she's stuck?'

'We don't know. Jeremy says that if she managed to get up, surely she can manage to get down. He thinks we should wait and see.'

Mandy knew that cats, even kittens of Amber's age, had excellent balance. On the other hand, it must be very cold up there on the roof. 'Have you tried to tempt her down?'

'Yes. I've just put out a saucer of milk on the front step. We've been calling her, but she takes no notice. What do you think we should do?'

'Keep trying,' Mandy decided. 'Try some food as well as milk. And tell Alex that cats usually come down when they're ready.'

'Right.' Mrs Hastings sounded reassured. 'It's just that at the moment we don't like anything to upset her. But anyway, you're probably right. We'll try the food, Mandy. Thank you very much.'

'That's OK. Will you ring us when Amber comes down?' Mandy would be uneasy until the problem was solved. She put down the phone and checked with Simon that she'd done the right thing.

'Fine,' he confirmed. He brought a list of fresh jobs for Mandy to be getting on with. 'Can you help me put a fresh dressing on the cocker spaniel's leg? Then we have to fit an Elizabethan collar to the border collie.'

'To stop him biting his stitches?' The farm dog had a jagged wound on his back. The collar made a cone shape around the dog's head so that he couldn't turn and tug at the affected area.

Simon nodded. They went ahead with the routine tasks, then, in the middle of the afternoon, Emily Hope popped her head around the door to check in with them. 'It's all go!' She looked busy but perfectly in control. The phone rang again. 'Get that, Mandy, would you?'

Mandy dashed into Reception. Perhaps it was Lisa Hastings with good news about Amber. 'Welford 703267.'

'Hi, Mandy, it's me!' James sounded far-off. 'Listen, you'll never guess what's happened.'

'Hi, James. You got lost?'

'No. We found the hospital OK. Father Christmas did his bit, even though I didn't actually see it. The nurses said my cold made me infectious. Anyway, all the kids got their presents. Dasher went into the ward with him. They loved it.'

'So?' She leaned sideways to look out of the window for a quick check on Rudolph.

'We're snowed in.'

'What?' Her jaw dropped.

'We're stuck here in Leeds. It's snowing like crazy, the roads are blocked, and we can't move!'

'Oh no!' If they didn't get back before

tomorrow, this would turn into a major crisis. 'For how long?'

'No one knows. They're out with the snow-plough and gritters, but you should see it, Mandy! People are saying that it might go on all day and all night!'

'Where are you exactly?'

'We're still at the hospital. Don was able to put Dasher out on the lawn, so he's happy. But he reckons we might not get back to Welford tonight.'

'What about tomorrow?' Christmas Eve; Father Christmas's special appearance. The collection for Alex. Her operation! Mandy's heart sank.

'We don't know. We hope we can make it. Don says to keep our fingers crossed. He said to ask how Rudolph is.'

'He's OK. He still looks down in the dumps, though. Listen, James...'

'Quick, Mandy. My money's running out.'

The phone line crackled. 'What are we going to do if you don't make it?'

Bip-bip-bip! The line buzzed and went dead. Mandy put down the phone with an empty click. She almost panicked. What a day! One crisis after another. And now, with just twenty-four hours to go to the big event, they had no sleigh, just one sick reindeer, and no Father Christmas!

Five

'Mandy, what on earth's the matter?' Her grandad strode into the surgery in his walking-boots, thick socks and a waxed jacket. He was on his way to the village, and had called in to see if they needed anything from the post office.

'Oh, Grandad; Father Christmas – Don McNab – is snowed in. He might not be able to get back for tomorrow night!'

'Well, I never!' Even Tom Hope was put off his stride. 'But we've already told everyone to come. They're even travelling over from Walton to see him. They're expecting us to put on a good show.' He sat for a moment on a chair in the waiting-room. He took off his thick gloves and ran a hand through his grey hair. 'And we're relying on that collection money to raise the final eight hundred pounds.'

'I know.' Mandy began to think. She stopped panicking, determined not to look on the black side. 'If the worst comes to the worst, at least we'll still have Rudolph.'

'But no sleigh and no Father Christmas,' Grandad groaned.

'No, and I suppose we don't even know if Rudolph will be better in time.' Mandy's nerve faltered as she glanced outside. It was the darkest time of the year. The light was already fading from an overcast sky. But at least it wasn't snowing here in Welford, and Rudolph was starting to scrape away at the snow to find the greenest grass shoots. 'But let's say he does make it,' she went on. 'Dad said it might be a twenty-four hour thing.'

'Yes?' Grandad looked weary. 'All that planning, and it could come to nothing,' he mumbled.

'Listen!' Mandy went and crouched beside him, willing him not to give in. 'Rudolph looks

OK; at least we'll have one reindeer!'

'And one is better than none?'

'Yes, and maybe the sleigh isn't that important. Or maybe someone like Mr Western or Mr Collins could lend us a trailer. We could decorate it with Christmas lights to make it look a bit like a sleigh!'

'A do-it-yourself effort?' Grandad picked up.

'Yes!' There was no stopping Mandy now. 'Ernie Bell's good at making things. Maybe we could get him to help. And it would be easy to get a stand-in Father Christmas. All we need is a big red suit with a hood and some white fur trimming. A big white beard, a sackful of presents . . . Her imagination ran on.

'And someone to wear it,' Grandad reminded her.

'Yes.' She stopped and looked him in the eye. 'Grandad . . .'

'Oh well, I don't know about that.' He coughed and stood up. 'I don't know that I'd be any good at dressing up. But you're right about the rest, Mandy. What we have to do now is mention it to a few people. I'm sure someone will volunteer straight away!'

* * *

'. . . I'll think about it,' Julian Hardy, the landlord at the Fox and Goose, listened to Grandad and Mandy's request. 'It's a bit short notice, but leave it with me.'

They'd left Animal Ark and walked into the village to look for a stand-in Father Christmas. The landlord was an obvious choice. The plan was for the procession to start outside the pub with traditional carols and the collection, before it moved up the road to Beechtrees.

'Go on, Dad!' John Hardy pressed him to be a good sport. 'They need someone to say yes right now.'

'I can sort out a costume for you, and a long white beard.' Sara, Julian's wife, was all for it too. 'It'll suit you!'

'Ho-ho-ho!' The landlord practised his laugh. 'No, it's not me,' he said with a frown. 'Besides, we'll be busy in the pub.'

'Oh, Dad!'

'Julian, please!' Sara encouraged.

'Let me think about it.' This was his final word for now, so Mandy and Tom Hope pressed on, across the square to Walter Pickard's corner house.

* * *

'. . . Me, dress up as Father Christmas?' Walter snorted. He'd invited them into his kitchen, but now he evidently wished he hadn't. 'I never heard anything so daft!'

'Wait a minute. Think about it.' Grandad Hope stood there, perfectly reasonable. 'You're the right age for the job, Walter.'

'And so are you,' he retorted.

'Yes, but I'm more on the management side of things. I'm a behind-the-scenes chap.'

Walter's eyebrows shot up. 'Oh, aye?'

'Yes. Whereas you're more the hands-on sort. I can just see you in a Father Christmas outfit, Walter. Besides, you wouldn't want to let everyone down, would you?'

Walter hummed and haahed. He coughed and shuffled. He said his rheumatism was bad, Tom was sick and needed full-time care.

'You won't be in the Fox and Goose for a pint tonight, then?' Grandad said with a sly wink at Mandy.

'Oh, I don't know about that,' came the instant response. He glowered at his visitors, unable to turn them down flat. 'Leave it with me,' he said as he showed them to the door. 'I'll mention it to Ernie. He's more your man!'

* * *

'. . . Father Christmas?' Adam Hope considered it. 'I'm a bit on the young side, aren't I?'

They'd bumped into him outside the post office on his way back from Sam Western's place. Customers came and went, rushing in to post late Christmas cards and to do last-minute errands. Mr Hope had stopped the Land-rover to offer Mandy and her grandfather a lift.

'I don't mind ringing Sam Western to ask if we can borrow his trailer,' he told them when he heard about the crisis. 'But I'm not so sure about playing the old man.'

'You'd be good at it,' Mandy pleaded. 'Wouldn't he, Grandad?'

'Brilliant. Just the right, friendly sort of chap.' But it looked as if Grandad Hope was beginning to think he would have to do the job himself after all. 'Look, if no one else seems keen, I suppose I could go home and get an outfit together before tomorrow night . . .'

'I might be out on call. Anything could happen between now and then.' Mandy's dad certainly wouldn't commit himself. 'Nice try, Mandy. I'll think about it.'

'What's the problem?' A familiar voice interrupted. Mrs Ponsonby appeared at the post-office door, ready to step into any breach. 'Do I take it that the real Father Christmas has gone missing?' She chortled at Mandy as she descended on to the pavement.

Mandy swallowed hard. Given half a chance, Mrs Ponsonby would step in and start bossing them around. 'He's stuck in Leeds,' she admitted. 'It's still snowing there. The roads are blocked.'

'Oh, dearie me!' And take charge Mrs Ponsonby did, standing there on the pavement with her two dogs, Toby and Pandora, both dressed in their little tartan jackets. 'We must do something!' She braced herself. The feathers in her red hat blew in the chilly breeze. Her round figure stood firm. 'We must find another!'

'Which is exactly what we're trying to do.' Mandy's grandad tried to get a word in.

Mrs Ponsonby swatted him away with her hand. 'Hush, Tom, I'm thinking . . . Yes, of course! Now look, you just leave it all to me!'

When Mandy and her grandfather had done

everything they could in the village, they went back to Animal Ark. It was past teatime, so Grandad continued down the lane to Lilac Cottage to hatch his own plans, while Mandy went into the house, tired and hungry.

'Which do you want first; the good news or the bad news?' her mum asked.

'The good news.' Mandy sighed and kicked off her boots. 'Go on, tell me that it's stopped snowing in Leeds and the roads are clear. Don is on his way back.'

'If only.' Emily Hope gave her a quick hug. 'But Rudolph is definitely on the mend. His temperature's down and he's eating normally.'

'Thank heavens for that.' Now the Christmas procession wouldn't be a complete flop. Rudolph could be the star of the show.

'Rudolph saves the day, just like in the song.' Adam Hope was on the phone. 'I'm ringing Susan Collins's dad to arrange for him to bring his trailer over first thing in the morning.'

'So what's the bad news?' Mandy asked warily. Her mum was dressed to go out into the snow in her hat and jacket.

'I just heard from Lisa Hastings at Beechtrees. Amber's still up on the roof.'

'Oh no! Didn't the food tempt her down?'

'Apparently not. And the temperature's dropped below freezing again. I said I'd go over to see if there was anything I could do.'

'I'll come!' Though she longed for a rest, Mandy immediately offered to help.

'Good. Come on, then. The sooner the better.'

So Mandy turned around, stuck her feet back into her boots and went with her mum.

'Tiring day?' Mrs Hope drove confidently down the narrow lane. The snow sparkled yellow under the headlights. When her four-wheel drive caught a low branch or a bush, a shower of soft snow fell to the ground.

Mandy nodded. 'Poor Amber. She's been up there for hours.'

'I know. And it's turned very cold again. I'm worried about hypothermia.' She glanced at Mandy. 'When body temperature falls below a certain level in an animal, or a person for that matter, it makes the victim sleepy. If it's bad, they become unconscious.'

'And Amber's only a kitten.'

'That makes it worse, I'm afraid. Kittens are more susceptible. They don't have as much body fat to protect them against the cold.'

Mandy bit her lip and tried not to think that far ahead.

Beechtrees came into sight as they drove past the Collinses' house. The main road was busy with traffic driving home from work or from last-minute Christmas shopping in Walton. Soon the car pulled up outside the bungalow.

'There she is; she's still up there!' Mandy scrambled out of the car as she spotted a tiny dark shape on the long slope of the white roof. Mr Hastings stood in the front garden. A ladder leaned against the side of the house.

'Let's hope it's not too late.' Emily Hope carried her heavy vet's bag into the porch. She had a quick word at the door with Mrs Hastings.

'We're sorry to drag you out,' Alex's mother began, 'but we've tried everything, short of actually climbing on to the roof. It's very slippery. And besides, Jeremy's afraid that it would scare the kitten even higher and make her lose her balance.'

'We don't mind.' Mrs Hope gave a reassuring smile. 'Where's Alex?'

'She's in her room. She's worried sick about poor Amber. No one knows how the kitten got on to the roof, but Alex is convinced it's her fault for not taking better care of her. She's crying her eyes out.'

'Tell her to try not to worry.' Emily Hope stepped back from the porch, and together with Mandy went to join Mr Hastings at the foot of the ladder.

'It's no good.' He shook his head. 'Every time I climb up there, she just creeps further away. I don't want to scare her into making a false move.'

Mandy craned her neck to see the tiny kitten. She could just make out a sorry bundle of fur shivering on the roof. She heard a feeble miaow. Amber was too frightened to move a muscle.

'How cold will she be up there?' Mr Hastings asked, anxious but helpless.

'Very cold. She'll get frostbite if she has to stay any longer.' Mrs Hope made a quick decision. 'Mandy and I will have a go at getting Amber down, but meanwhile I think you should call the RSPCA. They have the right equipment to get up there. Explain the situation to them, and see if they can come out right away!'

He nodded and ran inside. As he opened the door, Mandy caught a glimpse of William hovering in the hallway. It seemed he was curious to know what was going on, but was also trying to keep out of the way. The door closed again, and shut him inside.

'Let me go up the ladder, Mum,' Mandy said quickly. 'Amber knows me. She's more likely to come when I get up there and call her.'

Emily Hope checked the ladder. 'OK, but don't try anything risky when you get up there. I don't want you climbing on to the roof under any circumstances. Got that?' She knew Mandy would be willing to risk it unless she ordered her not to.

Mandy had to agree. She would have to rely on coaxing Amber down.

'Good luck,' her mum said, holding the ladder firm as Mandy set foot on the first metal rung.

She counted the steps; six, seven, eight. At nine, her head reached roof level. She peered up the snowy slope to the ridge. Amber sat and shivered against the chimney stack. Her eyes gleamed orange in the dark. 'Here, Amber!' Mandy edged up another rung. The kitten backed away.

'That's far enough, Mandy!' her mum warned

from below. 'If she won't come when you call, we'll leave it to the RSPCA!'

Mandy leaned against the guttering and reached out with both hands. Her legs had begun to tremble. The icy wind whipped up loose snow and blew it in her face. 'Amber, don't be scared. Come this way!'

In her confusion, Amber thought that Mandy's outstretched arms meant danger. She edged back again, almost lost her footing on the snow-covered ridge and half slipped from sight. Mandy gasped. With a struggle, the kitten found her balance and cowered against the chimney stack.

'Any good?' Mrs Hope called.

'No!' Mandy looked desperately along the treacherous surface. The roof was smooth and white except for two raised squares where windows had been built in for extra light. These too were snow-covered, but they gave Mandy an idea. 'I'm coming down!' Forcing her trembling legs into action, she climbed down the ladder.

'What next?' Emily Hope looked at her watch. 'Where's the RSPCA got to?'

'I'm going to try from inside!' Mandy ran to

explain to Mr and Mrs Hastings. 'Can you open the roof windows from inside the house?'

Jeremy Hastings nodded. 'They work on hinges and lift up. Come and see!'

He led her to Alex's bedroom.

'Mandy, please get Amber down!' The little girl sat huddled on her bed, crying at the thought of Amber freezing to death.

She put on a brave show of confidence. 'Don't worry, we'll get her back for you.' She was shocked by Alex's pale, tear-stained face, her tiny, distressed voice.

'Don't let her die, please!'

'Now Alex, we're all doing our best, love.' Jeremy Hastings looked round the room for something to stand on.

She sobbed quietly and hid her face as her dad put a chair in the middle of the room and began to lever at the snow covered roof in the sloping ceiling.

Mandy waited impatiently, hoping that the noise wouldn't frighten the kitten outside.

'No good, it's frozen solid.' Mr Hastings gave up and jumped to the floor.

'What about the other one?' Mandy had seen the shape of a second window.

'In William's room!' He left Alex crying and ran next door, bursting in without knocking.

Mandy followed. What was William making of all this? She saw him on his bed, pale and silent, pretending to read a book, but obviously scared. She stood under the skylight while Mr Hastings ran for a chair to stand on. Looking down, she saw that the fawn carpet had a darker stain; a patch of wet about ten centimetres across.

William followed her gaze. He slammed his book shut and glowered.

Had water leaked in through the window frame? Mandy looked up. Or had snow drifted in through the open window? This window was lower, just out of reach. She shot another glance at Alex's brother, who went whiter still. His lip began to quiver as he heard his dad coming back.

'William?' It struck Mandy all at once; that was how Amber had got stuck on the roof. The boy had opened the window and put her there on purpose! Then he'd slammed it shut and locked her out!

'Don't tell!' he whispered, guilty, terrified.

Mr Hastings dashed in and put the chair over

the wet patch without noticing it. He climbed up on it. This time, the window opened easily. He eased it up and propped it into position. 'Come on, Mandy, take a look. See if you can coax Amber down from here.'

Recovering from her shock, she stood on the chair and peered out. She was closer to Amber, but still not able to reach. The kitten saw her, but this time she didn't react. She blinked and shivered, but didn't try to escape.

Mandy knew the signs. This was worse than before; Amber was so cold that she was growing sleepy. But it was the kind of sleep before she

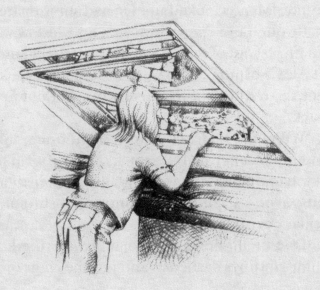

fell unconscious and froze to death. 'Amber, here!' Mandy cried. She tried desperately to slither on to the roof.

'Careful!' Mr Hastings yelled.

Out on the road, an RSPCA van pulled up at last. From her vantage point, she could see two men rush into the Hastings' garden with special roof ladders. They scrambled up the side of the bungalow, one after the other, laid the roof ladder flat on top of the snow and pushed it into position.

Amber saw it and gave a cry. She darted away, along the ridge of the roof, almost slipped and fell.

'Watch out!' Mandy warned. The first man began to scale the roof. 'She might fall!'

But it was now or never. If the kitten stayed out any longer, she might die. Mandy hoped and prayed that the men would succeed where she had failed.

But terror jerked Amber into action. She made another run, further out of reach. She looked round, eyes wide with fright. There, just above, was an overhanging branch from one of the tall trees in the garden. The kitten saw it and crouched. The man hesitated. Then he lunged to grab her.

Amber jumped. She sprang up on to the nearest branch. It dipped and swayed. The kitten hung on.

'I've lost her!' the man shouted. Outside, someone else yelled, and the traffic on the road rumbled by. The dark shadow of the tree had swallowed Amber.

'Quick!' Mandy slid back into the bedroom, bringing a shower of loose snow with her. She ran out through the hall into the porch. Her mum stood with her bag, ready to treat the kitten. 'She's up in the tree. We can't see her!'

'Bring a torch!' Emily Hope told Jeremy Hastings. They ran to the base of the tree.

'Shine it up into the branches!' The RSPCA man held his own torch. The yellow beams shone through the dark.

'She's up there somewhere!' Mandy whispered. 'She has to be!'

But though the RSPCA men brought their ladder and climbed once more, they couldn't find Amber.

'She can't just disappear!' Frantic, Mandy ran into the road to see if she could see Amber from out there. The moon shone through the bare branches; there was no sign.

'Watch the cars!' Mr Hastings warned.

Mandy kept close to the side, searching the road just in case the kitten had lost her balance and fallen. Again, nothing!

Amber's mighty leap from rooftop to tree had ended in mystery. They searched and searched, but the kitten seemed to have vanished into thin air!

Six

'What shall I tell Alex?' Mr Hastings asked as he clicked off his torch.

They felt empty and cold. The men from the RSPCA had stacked their ladders on top of the van and driven away from Beechtrees.

'I think we should tell her the truth.' Mandy's mum offered to help him explain.

They trudged into the house. Mrs Hastings brought Alex from her room and they broke the news that Amber was lost. There were tearful questions; 'How can she be? Isn't she stuck on the roof? Where is she now?' The grown-ups were gentle, but they had to admit that they had failed.

'At least until it gets light,' her mum told her. 'Then we can begin to look again. We'll be able to see more in the daylight.'

'But it's so cold!' Alex shivered with fear. 'Why can't we try to find her *now?*'

'We *have* looked for a long time,' Mr Hastings began. But he saw the look in Alex's green eyes. 'OK, I'll try again.'

Mandy said she would go with him, while Mrs Hastings and her own mum did their best to calm Alex.

'William, come and give us a hand,' Jeremy Hastings called from the front porch.

The boy's bedroom door opened slowly. When he saw Mandy, he closed it quickly again.

'What's got into him?' His father was impatient. 'As if we didn't have enough to worry about, without William going into a sulk.'

Mandy waited while he went to fetch his son. William appeared reluctantly, grumbling about having to go out in the cold. He avoided Mandy's gaze.

'It isn't even my kitten,' he complained, as his dad made him put on his jacket and boots.

'But Alex is upset. Don't you want to help us find Amber for her sake?'

William screwed his mouth up tight. He said nothing.

'Come on, try and put someone else first for a change.' Mr Hastings handed them each a torch and they went outside. They searched behind bushes along a low wall, across the lawn where the two snowmen still stood, gleaming white in the moonlight.

'Let's look for paw-prints,' Mandy suggested. She directed her torchbeam along the ground. 'If Amber did fall out of the tree and manage to run off, we should soon be able to pick up her trail.'

For a while, their search had a new purpose. Surely Mandy was right; the kitten would have left some evidence in the snow. But the minutes ticked by. They looked on the lawn, then under the beech tree for the telltale prints. Mr Hastings even went up his ladder to investigate the roof for fresh signs. He had no luck up there either.

'I'm freezing!' William moaned. He sniffled and whined. 'My toes hurt! I can't feel my fingers!'

'Well, just think how cold Amber must be!' Mr Hastings refused to let him retreat into the house. 'Now go with Mandy and look on the road. Watch out for cars!'

'It's all clear,' Mandy called. She stood at the gate, shining her torch along the wall top where the tree branches hung over the road. 'Can you see any prints?' she asked William.

He scowled. 'No. And it's not my fault if the stupid cat goes missing! Why can't Alex look after her properly?'

Mandy bit her tongue. She hated it when people called animals stupid. All of a sudden she had to say something. 'Listen, William!' She pulled him to one side and whispered urgently.

'Let go! What?'

'Are you sure it's not your fault that Amber went missing? What about that patch of melted snow on your carpet?'

'Don't blame me. I was only trying to rescue the stupid thing before Mum went and rang you lot!' He looked at her at last, eyes flashing angrily. 'Anyway, I know you won't believe me. No one ever does. They never blame Alex. It's always me!' He pulled his sleeve free and ran into the garden. Mandy quickly followed.

She saw William jump the low wall on to the lawn. He headed straight for the snowmen which he and James had built, threw himself at the nearest one and began shoving and kicking it until it toppled and shattered. It lay in frozen lumps. Soon he had destroyed the second one too.

'There!' He rounded on her, as his father came running down the path. 'That's what I think of stupid snowmen. And I hope you never find Amber! I hope she freezes to death!'

'He didn't really mean it,' Mrs Hope explained as she drove Mandy home.

'He sounded as if he did.' Mandy had been shocked by the outburst. In the end, Mrs Hastings had come out and taken William inside.

'He is only seven, remember. And his family has a lot of problems at the moment.'

'Yes, and William's making them worse.' Mandy couldn't forgive his cruel taunt about Amber. She sat looking out at the snow-covered hillside, staring disaster in the face. For one thing, there were the snags over Father Christmas. Gran and Grandad's fund-raising treat could well fall completely flat. For another, Alex was so upset about Amber that she might be too ill to enjoy the procession even if it did take place. And then of course, there was the kitten out all night in the cold.

'I'm sure he doesn't mean to make things worse,' her mum insisted. 'I don't think he can help it, poor boy.' She swung down their lane, talking things through. 'It must be hard for him, having a little sister who gets all the attention. Alex is ill, so naturally her mum and dad worry about her. They don't have much time to spare for William at the moment. I expect he feels left out.'

'Jealous?' Mandy considered it for the first time. 'But that didn't mean he had to go and spoil the snowmen. That doesn't make sense.'

'Sometimes things don't make sense.' They turned into their own drive and pulled up in the yard.

'Mum . . . ?' Frowning, Mandy unclicked her seatbelt. 'I know what you mean. William's getting his own back.'

'Yes. But he's having to take it out on things that never did anything to him in the first place. Like the snowmen.'

'And Amber?' Mandy wondered out loud. William had denied it, but the suspicion lingered that he was the one who had put the kitten on the roof.

'Possibly.' Mrs Hope listened quietly to the full story, as Mandy saw it. She sighed. 'Oh dear, I hope not. The poor boy must be feeling wretched.'

'Poor *Alex*, poor *Amber*!' If it was true, William had taken out his problem on the thing his sister loved best. And now an innocent animal was suffering because of it.

'Cheer up!' Adam Hope greeted them with a smile. 'Don't tell me you didn't see them out in the yard?'

Mandy shook her head wearily. 'No. Who?'

'Not who; what. The van and trailer. Don's back!'

'Och aye, I'm back all right.' The wiry Scotsman came downstairs in T-shirt, jeans and bare feet. 'I've had a long, hot bath and now I'm ready to put my feet up in front of the TV.'

'Is Dasher with you?' It took a while to sink in. The last Mandy had heard was that the trailer was stuck in a snowdrift outside a Leeds hospital.

'Aye, and young James. All home safe and sound.' Don's face was shiny red after his bath. 'Now where did I put those trainers?' He

scratched his head and began to search the kitchen.

'But how did you get here?' For a moment Mandy had a vision of the reindeer rising magically above the rooftops drawing the sleigh.

'The snow-ploughs dug us out. They did a great job. By teatime they had the traffic moving again. We couldn't get a message through to you, so we headed for home. It's a good wee story, though. He chuckled over it. 'Now where *did* I put those shoes?'

'At least I won't have to get dressed up in that red suit.' Mr Hope sounded relieved. He made

Mandy sit down to a big plateful of beans on toast. 'You had us worried for a while, Don. Mandy's grandad has been all over the village trying to round up a stand-in.'

'And no one wanted to do it,' Mandy added. She tucked into her supper, glad that at least one of the major crisis was over. 'Everyone said, "Let me think about it", which means, "No", doesn't it? But anyway, Rudolph's better and you're back.'

'No problem!' Don was cheery as ever. 'Maybe I left them in my bag,' he muttered to himself. He shuffled off in bare feet, upstairs to the spare room. They heard a few thumps and clomps as he came back down; shoes on but unlaced, and wearing a puzzled frown. 'That's not like me. I'm usually a very organised sort of person!'

Mandy rolled her eyes at her mum and dad. Don was many good things, but organised wasn't one of them. 'What have you lost?'

'Och, I wouldn't say "lost" exactly. More mislaid. Aye, but I could have sworn I put them in my bag.'

'Your shoes? They're on your feet, Don.' Mandy broke it to him gently.

'Och, no, not my shoes. No, I'm talking about

Father Christmas's clothes; the old gentleman's best red suit and black boots. I told him I'd spruce them up for Christmas Eve, so he left them with me. I've looked, and I can't find them anywhere!'

'He left them at the hospital,' Adam Hope confirmed as he came in to say goodnight to Mandy. 'The nursing manager just called and left a message. Father Christmas's suit is neatly folded on a bed in an empty side ward!'

Mandy made a noise halfway between a groan and a giggle.

'Yes, and you thought *I* was absent-minded!' He sat down for a moment on the edge of her bed. 'Your mum says you've had a hard day?'

She nodded. 'We looked everywhere for Amber, Dad, but we just couldn't find her. What do you think can have happened to her?' She knew that she wouldn't sleep for worrying.

Her dad shrugged. 'I don't know for sure, but let's try and work it out. Because one thing's for sure; a cat really can't just vanish. So, first off, you say she definitely jumped off the roof?'

'Yes, into the tree by the wall. We saw her

land, but it was so dark among the branches that we lost sight of her.'

'And she's absolutely definitely not still up there?'

'No. So where can she be?'

'Well . . .' He spoke gently. 'We have to face that fact that Amber might have fallen.'

Mandy scrunched up her face and closed her eyes. She didn't want to hear this.

'No, listen, love. Say she did fall; after all, it was dark and she was very frightened. But you know cats have this amazing ability to land on their feet. We call it a head-on-body righting reflex.'

She opened her eyes to look at him. 'Meaning what?'

'It works like this. A cat falls from a height. First it twists so that the top of its head faces upwards. Then the neck and body line up in the reflex action so that the cat falls feet first. It only takes milliseconds, and lo and behold, she lands safely. One of her nine lives is saved!'

Mandy took a deep breath. 'Do you think that's what happened to Amber?'

'It's possible. She falls and lands the right way up, no damage done. Then as quick as she can she darts for cover, waits for all the fuss to die down.'

'Yes. Maybe she didn't like the torches and all the noise.' Mandy pictured the kitten tucked safely out of harm's way, sheltered from the wind and waiting for the all-clear. Tomorrow morning the Hastings would open their front door and discover her, sitting on the mat and miaowing for her breakfast. 'I just hope she found a nice warm place to hide.'

'Me too.' Her dad stood up and turned off the light. 'After a day like today, we deserve a bit of luck. So try not to worry too much, OK?'

The door closed and left the room in darkness. Mandy tried to sleep. But one thing bothered her. If her dad was right, and Amber had landed safely, why hadn't they found any paw-prints in the snow? Mandy tussled with the problem until well after midnight. No paw-prints, no evidence, nothing. Poor little Amber; it seemed that she had simply been spirited away.

Seven

Gran turned up at Animal Ark before breakfast, armed with scissors, sewing-pins and an armful of old red curtain material. 'We'll just have to make do and mend!' she cried, seizing hold of Don. She measured him for a replacement Father Christmas suit. 'I expect Santa Claus is about the same size as you,' she said with a wink.

'Aye, though he's a wee bit fatter around the waist.' Don patted his stomach.

As usual, Mandy played along. She helped Gran get him ready for the grand procession that evening.

They laid the fabric flat on the kitchen table,

cut and shaped it, then Gran began to sew to the whirr of the machine, making tucks, seams and fastenings. By nine o'clock, Don was trying on the finished article.

'Beard?' Gran stood back to judge the effect.

'Cotton wool!' Mandy ran to the surgery. She dived through the busy waiting-room, grabbed a pack from the cupboard, and raced back to the house. By hook or by crook they would be ready for the big event.

'Boots?' Gran was almost finished. The beard was a miracle of cardboard, glue and cotton wool, with elastic loops to hook over the ears.

'Dad's wellies!' Mandy sprang to fetch them. Then, when they were satisfied and Don had gone outside to groom Rudolph and Dasher so that they would look their best for that evening, she rang James to see if he would come along to Beechtrees with her.

'What time is it? Have you rung them yet?' James inquired sleepily.

'No, not yet.' Mandy had been putting it off. 'And they haven't rung us either.' Her hopes that Amber would turn up on the doorstep of the bungalow were fading. She knew that the Hastings would have telephoned with any good news about the kitten. 'I wondered if you would come and help us look.' She would be glad if he said yes. James was brilliant in a crisis. He kept a clear head and always came up with bright ideas.

'Sure. What time?'

'In half an hour.'

'See you there.' He was alert now, and didn't waste time talking.

In fact, he was at the bungalow before her. When Mandy arrived, he was already looking for the lost kitten with Mrs Hastings. Mr Hastings had gone to work at the tennis club, and William and Alex were inside.

'How is she?' Mandy asked.

'Not quite so upset as yesterday. But she's very sad,' Mrs Hastings told them. 'I can't think of anything to cheer her up. She's completely lost interest in Christmas.'

Mandy knew how Alex must feel. Even making Father Christmas's outfit with Gran hadn't stopped her from worrying about Amber. 'Shall I go in and see her?'

'Would you mind, Mandy? You're the only person Alex is interested in talking to right now. I'm afraid she sees you as some kind of heroine, like Superwoman!' Mrs Hastings gave a sad smile and led Mandy and James through the hallway.

James stayed in the kitchen while Mandy tiptoed into Alex's quiet room. The curtains were drawn, and a dim lamp shone. All around the walls, pictures of animals seemed to stare down at the sick little girl who lay motionless in bed.

'Hi, Alex.' Mandy sat close by. There was a full glass of water on the bedside table, next to an unopened book.

Alex turned her head. When she spoke, her voice was a whisper. 'Hello, Mandy. Guess what, I don't think Father Christmas read my letter.'

'Why not?' Mandy saw now what Mr and Mrs Hastings meant when they insisted that Alex must be kept calm. Being upset drained her of her strength. She lay white as a ghost.

'I wrote and asked him for a collar for Amber; one with a little bell.'

'Well, you never know.' She tried to sound cheerful. 'He might bring you one. He hasn't delivered his presents yet, remember!'

Alex's eyes filled with tears. 'No, but if he got my note, he'd know I've got a kitten. Then he wouldn't let Amber get lost, would he?'

'I don't think even Father Christmas can do anything about a kitten going missing,' Mandy explained gently.

'But he knows everything! He knows what we'd all like for Christmas. He can even fly through the air with his reindeer. He must know about Amber!'

Mandy nodded. 'Well, maybe he does.'

Alex had a sudden idea. She wiped her eyes and looked at Mandy. 'Yes, and maybe he's looking after her for me! That could be where Amber is right now – with Father Christmas!'

'I hope so,' Mandy whispered, before Mrs Hastings came in to give Alex her medicine, Mandy crept out of the room to join James in the kitchen.

After a few minutes Mrs Hastings followed. 'She's sleeping,' she reported. 'It's an extra strain on her heart when she's upset. She isn't strong enough to take it.' It was Alex's mother's turn to brush away a tear.

'Come on, let's start,' James suggested, ready to take up the search. They went out on to the porch.

'I dread what sort of time we'll have if we don't

find this kitten.' Mrs Hastings scanned the trampled lawn. 'We've been over and over the ground, but there's still no sign.'

James agreed. 'I thought we might find prints in the snow, but it's all trodden down, so even if there was a track last night, it's disappeared by now.'

'I did look,' Mandy told him. 'And I couldn't see one. William and I even searched out on the road.' She glanced at the house to see the small, pale face and ginger hair of Alex's brother staring solemnly at them through the window.

James studied the beech tree where Amber had last been seen. Then he went out to look at the road, which was quiet at this time of day. He stood under the overhanging branches and looked up, pushing his hair from his forehead. 'Who saw her up there?'

'Let's think; me, Mum, Mr Hastings, and the two men from the RSPCA.'

'And the people driving by,' James suggested. 'If Amber managed to scramble down the tree on this side, then ran off, maybe someone in a car caught sight of her as well?'

Mandy nodded. 'All we need is one clue to

find out which way she went. But how do we find out if anybody saw her?'

'We could ask in the village. There would be plenty of people around on Christmas Eve, doing their last-minute shopping. It's worth a try.'

Mrs Hastings agreed. 'You two go and ask. I'll stay here and make some notices to stick up on trees and gateposts to say we've lost a kitten. I'll get Alex and William to help me.' She seemed glad to have something to do.

So Mandy and James went into Welford. They called at the McFarlanes and the Fox and Goose. They saw James's dad talking in the square to Mrs Collins. They saw Ernie Bell and Walter Pickard.

'Tom's right as rain!' Walter called. 'Back to normal, as bossy as ever!'

They passed the message; the Hastings' kitten, Amber, was lost in the snow. Had anyone seen a stray tortoiseshell with bright golden eyes? Each time the answer came back: 'No, sorry. But we will keep a lookout!' Even the people who remembered driving past the bungalow at about the right time hadn't seen a thing.

They asked the Parker Smythes and Sam

Western, as well as the farmer from Greystones, David Gill. All promised to do their best, but they shook their heads as if to say, 'What chance does a little kitten have out in the freezing cold at this time of year?'

By lunchtime Mandy and James had done all they could. They headed back, past the square, where Julian Hardy from the pub was stringing up big Christmas lights. 'Ready for Father Christmas,' he said. 'I hear everything's going ahead?'

Mandy nodded. Her legs were weary from tramping through the snow. And so far, all for nothing. They were no nearer to finding Amber. She forgot to mention to Mr Hardy that Don McNab and Dasher were back in Welford, ready for tonight's procession.

'Sara's busy baking mince-pies. And John's made christingle candles for the kids. The vicar's bringing a tape of Christmas carols, and I'll rig up loudspeakers so we can all sing along.'

Everyone was pulling out all the stops in aid of Alex's lifesaving trip to America. Mandy and James watched for a while, then went on, deep in thought. 'You know something?' Mandy said,

'Unless we find Amber, I don't think Alex will go!'

'For her operation?' James began to see how important the missing kitten was. 'You mean, she's just too upset?'

Mandy sighed and nodded. 'And too ill to travel. Come on, we'd better go and see what's happening.'

'If only *I*'d seen something.' James strode along beside her. 'Don and I drove along this road yesterday teatime, on our way back from Leeds.'

'Along with a hundred other cars.' She was beginning to feel that it was like looking for a needle in a haystack.

'Well, it looks like William is trying to help at last.' James spotted him in the garden. William climbed the wall and stood, watching them approach. As they drew near, he dropped to the ground and ran to meet them.

'Alex is even more sick! They've fetched the doctor.' His eyes were wide and scared. 'Did you find the kitten?'

Looking up the drive, they saw a red car, and the front door of the bungalow standing open. A tall woman came out carrying a dark bag.

She stopped to talk earnestly to Mrs Hastings. The moment William spotted them, he ducked behind the wall. 'That's her,' he told them. 'That's the doctor!'

They waited until the woman had got into her car, backed out of the drive and driven off. By this time, William was shaking from head to foot.

'I never meant her to get sick!' He trembled and fought back the tears, refusing to go any nearer to his house. The front door was closed, the bungalow strangely quiet.

'Just like you never meant Amber to get lost in the snow?' Mandy asked quietly.

James stepped back in surprise. William hung his head. 'I only wanted her to be on the roof for a bit. I didn't know she wouldn't come down again.' He mumbled and choked over how his plan had gone wrong.

'You mean, *you* put Amber up there?' James was stunned.

Mandy nodded. 'I thought so. Listen.' She knew the whole story would soon come tumbling out.

'Yes, but I thought I could get her down again. They'd all be looking for her, and I'd be the one who saved her, see?'

'But it didn't work out.' Instead of rescuing the kitten and being the hero, William had to watch Amber climb out of reach on the roof, then get too scared to move, slowly growing colder and colder as night fell. 'Why didn't you tell someone?'

'I was frightened,' he confessed. 'I thought Amber was going to die because of me.' Tears welled up and rolled down his cheeks.

'Look, never mind that now.' James knew there was no point crying over it. 'At least we know how it happened.'

Mandy wondered how James could be so kind. She found it hard to forgive William. But the little boy looked miserable as he realised just what he'd done, and Mandy remembered what her mum had said; William was feeling left out. He was a lonely child who knew he'd done wrong. 'We won't tell anyone,' she whispered. 'Don't cry any more. Just help us to find Amber!'

William sniffed and dried his eyes on his cuff. 'I don't want to go in,' he pleaded.

'OK.' James was practical. 'Let's stay outside and look.'

'Again!' Mandy stood at the gates, hands on hips. It almost drove her mad to think how often they'd gone over this ground since Amber had disappeared.

But William shook his head. 'No!' he insisted. He pulled back as James tried to persuade him to come into the garden.

'Why not? The least you can do is help us look!' For the first time, James sounded cross.

'I can't. Anyway, there isn't any point!'

Mandy turned. 'Don't, James. What's wrong, William?' She suspected there was more to come.

'Amber's not here.'

'How come? Did you see what happened?'

Slowly he nodded. 'I was looking out of the window. She was in the tree. Everyone was using ladders and torches, but I knew it wasn't any use.'

'Why not? What did you see?' She longed to shake the truth out of him, but she forced herself to be patient.

William stood at the roadside, pointing up at the tree. 'She was in that branch, there. I saw her. I shouted, but you didn't hear because there was too much noise.' There was a long pause. 'Amber fell.'

'Where? Into the road?' James was the one to prompt him, as Mandy held her breath.

'No. She fell on to a sort of truck. I saw her slip from the branch. The next second the truck went past the gate and I saw Amber on top of it, hanging on.'

'Alive?' Mandy gasped.

He nodded. 'The truck drove on. I couldn't stop it.'

James's mind flew ahead. Mandy was dazed, but overjoyed that Amber had survived the fall. 'What kind of truck?' he asked.

'A grey one. It was a kind of trailer.'

James stared. 'What was pulling the trailer?'

Mandy grabbed James's arm, waiting in suspense for the reply.

'A big van, a dirty white one. It was covered in snow. I've never seen it before.'

They gasped. 'Don!' they said together.

'The reindeer's trailer!' Now, at this moment, Mandy could have hugged William. Here was the clue they needed. 'Amber fell on top of it!'

'It looks like it,' James breathed. 'The kitten must have driven home with Don and me!'

'To Animal Ark!' Mandy cried. 'Oh, James, Alex was right; Father Christmas has been looking after Amber all along!'

Eight

'William saw what happened to Amber!' Mandy told Mrs Hastings, so excited that she could hardly get the words out. 'At last we've picked up a lead we can follow!'

Mrs Hastings went straight away to tell Alex the latest news while William slipped quietly back into the house. 'I won't get her hopes up too high just yet,' Alex's mum said. 'But at least this should help to cheer her up.'

'We hope!' James whispered to Mandy as they set off down the road, as fast as they could, towards Animal Ark.

* * *

Back at Animal Ark, Mandy and James found the reindeer's trailer standing in the yard. Its doors hung open and the ramp was down. They nearly fell over themselves getting inside it. Their feet thumped up the ramp, and they almost tumbled over.

But, once inside, they soon realised that the dark trailer was empty. Mandy had longed for it to be simple. She had hoped Amber had clung on to the top of the trailer and during the journey home had clambered inside to safety – to spend the night in the warm straw. But no; the trailer was bare. No kitten, not even any straw.

'Don must have cleaned it out,' James said, his voice flat.

'Let's make sure.' Mandy took one last look round, then went out, and hoisted herself up on to a ledge to look on top. There was no kitten there, but something caught her eyes. 'James, come and look at this!'

James joined her. Together they peered on to the snowy roof of the trailer.

'See there.' She pointed.

Frozen into the deep snow was a trail of paw-prints which led from a scuffed patch.

'You think that's where Amber fell?'

'Yes, then she crept to that far edge, there.'

'Well, at least we know William's telling the truth,' James agreed. 'But that's not to say that Amber stayed there all the way back here.' He jumped down and tried to think what to do next.

'Let's ask Don if he knows anything.' Mandy caught sight of him in the compound with the two reindeer. 'Don!'

He waved as she ran across.

'Don, did you just muck out the trailer?'

'I did.' He hummed cheerfully. Rudolph was enjoying a grooming session ready for the big night. Dasher nibbled at a dish of sugar beet.

'Did you see anything in there?' Again she was in such a rush that the words tumbled out. 'Like a kitten, for instance?'

'Whoa, slow down!' His eyes crinkled with amusement. Mandy hopped from foot to foot, and now James came running. Rudolph grunted and nudged at Don's hand. 'Aye, steady on, Rudi. I haven't forgotten you!'

'A brown and black tortoiseshell kitten with amber eyes!' Mandy gave a full description to a mystified Don.

'Aye, as it happens, I did.'

'Oh!' Mandy clasped her hands together. 'Oh, Don, where is she? What did you do with her?'

'Well, I didn't do anything with her.' He scratched his head. 'I went into the box and there she was curled up in the straw, cosy as you like. Cheeky wee thing.'

'You didn't chase her away?' James asked anxiously.

'Och, what do you take me for? It was a pity to disturb her; she'd found a grand spot for a wee nap. No, I went off to fetch her a saucer of milk, but wouldn't you just know it? The minute I turned my back, off she ran.' He shrugged and started again on Rudolph's thick coat. 'She's a wicked wee cat, right enough.'

Mandy stared. 'She ran off?' she faltered.

'Aye, but don't worry. Kittens don't stray far from home. You'll soon have her back safe and sound.'

'No,' James cut in. 'Amber doesn't belong to Mandy. She doesn't live here at Animal Ark.'

'But I thought you said you were looking for her?' Don stood up straight and wrinkled his forehead.

'For someone else,' James explained. 'Did you see which way she ran?' Of course, Don couldn't realise how important this was. They'd been so near to finding Amber, yet now they'd lost her again.

He sighed. 'I didn't. She nipped away when my back was turned. I just got on and mucked out as usual. I never gave the wee cat a second thought.'

Mandy hid her disappointment. 'Never mind. Thanks, Don.'

'Och, I've a feeling I've let you down,' he apologised.

'No.' She managed to smile. 'At least we know Amber was here.'

'How long ago?' James fitted together all the information he could gather.

'Half an hour. Maybe a wee bit longer.'

Mandy nodded at James. 'Then she can't have gone far!' she said, jutting out her chin and looking across the yard. The hunt for Amber was on.

In the small village of Welford, news of the missing kitten travelled fast.

'Little Alex Hastings is ill with worry, poor child!' Mrs Ponsonby spread the word. She'd heard it from Emily Hope when she went into the surgery with snuffly Pandora. She told Mrs McFarlane that the kitten was still alive. 'Isn't that wonderful? And wouldn't it be the best Christmas present in the world if we all helped to find her?' Warm-hearted in spite of her bossy manner, Mrs Ponsonby raised a search party.

'I suppose I've nothing better to do.' Ernie Bell hid his willingness to help beneath a grumpy surface. He picked up a shovel from his garden shed and set off for Animal Ark, ready to dig through snowdrifts and do his very best.

Walter Pickard, not to be outdone, went with him. 'We can't have the little lass making herself poorly over it, can we?'

And John Hardy, the serious, studious son of the landlord, went along with Susan Collins. Even Brandon Gill, the shy boy from Greystones Farm, got to hear about Amber and tramped across the snowy fields to Mandy's house. Soon a dozen people, young and old, were helping James and Mandy in the search for Amber.

'We must spread out in different directions!' Mrs Ponsonby was wearing a bright pink anorak with a white fake-fur trim. She had a master plan. 'Mandy and James have checked the house thoroughly, so we can be sure that the kitten has gone further afield. We will split into twos and search the lane with a fine-tooth comb. Now Mandy, please give a detailed description.' She clapped her hands smartly. 'Attention everyone, please!'

Mandy blushed as she gave the information. 'Amber is a black and brown tortoiseshell with golden-orange eyes. Her tail is mostly black. There's a flash of white on one back leg. She's five months old.' Even as she spoke, she realised that the short daylight hours would soon draw to a close. They must get the search underway as soon as possible.

They left it to Mrs Ponsonby to divide people into pairs. 'Walter, you come along with me!' she instructed, after she'd sent all the others off.

Mandy raised her eyebrows. James breathed a sigh of relief. Walter got no chance to object.

'Go on, Mandy. You and James head for Lilac Cottage. See if your grandparents have seen or heard anything useful!' Mrs Ponsonby implied that the two of them were slacking.

They shot off, leaving Walter to be bossed around by her, passing Brandon and Susan who had been sent to look in the field opposite Animal Ark.

'Here!' Susan said, suddenly excited. She pointed to a track that led right across the field. 'A set of footprints!'

James and Mandy jumped the ditch to peer over the wall.

Brandon stopped to examine them. 'A fox,' he said quietly, shaking his head.

'Oh, Brandon, are you sure?' Susan was dismayed. She clung on to her discovery. 'But they look like cat prints to me!'

'Fox,' he said stubbornly. 'They're too heavy for a kitten.'

Susan sighed and gave in. Mandy and James jumped back into the lane and went on. The snow still lay deep and pretty as a Christmas card along all the wall-tops and gates, weighing down the dark tree branches. By the time they reached the cottage, they'd passed Ernie, John Hardy and Mr Hastings, who'd rushed over from work the moment he heard the news.

'Thanks, you two!' He raised his head and called after him. 'You don't know how much we appreciate this!'

'Thank us later,' Mandy told him.

'When we find Amber!' James added.

At Lilac Cottage Grandad stood holding the gate open for them. 'Come on. Your gran and I have been having a good scout around, but no luck so far, I'm afraid.'

It was the same old story; everyone doing their best but getting nowhere.

'That kitten certainly has a knack of vanishing!' Gran was in the front garden, looking under benches and behind bare trellises where, in the summer, roses grew.

'Poor thing. It must be a big cold world out here for her.' Grandad pictured her lost and frightened. It made James and Mandy concentrate even harder.

'Here, Mandy!' James called at last. His warm breath turned to clouds of steam as he trod carefully amongst Mr Hope's vegetable garden at the back of the cottage. 'Come and look!'

Mandy walked delicately between the mysterious white humps and clumps. Under the snow lay Grandad's precious rhubarb and fruit bushes. Her footsteps were the first to spoil the smooth surface of the carefully tended ground.

James crouched by a round water butt at the bottom of the garden. The barrel was covered over with a thick layer of ice, but it was the base that he was interested in. There, around the back of the barrel, leading along the garden boundary towards the house, was a beautiful, clear set of paw-prints!

'What do you think?' he breathed. 'Not a fox's this time?'

'Definitely not! Not so close to the house.' She followed the track to see where it led. 'Anyway, they're too small for a fox.'

Excited now, they followed the trail on to the patio. They lost it, then found it again. The prints lead along the patio, straight up to the sliding glass doors.

Mandy turned to James. 'What now?'

He shook his head. 'It looks like she went inside.'

'But who would let her in? Gran and Grandad would have mentioned it.' Doubts came to the surface; doubts that she didn't want to admit.

James pressed his face to the glass and peered inside. 'Uh, Mandy . . .' he said dully.

She forced herself to look. *Please let it be Amber!* she prayed. But there, sitting peacefully in his favourite armchair, carefully grooming behind his ears, was the sleek grey shape of Smoky, Gran and Grandad's own precious cat.

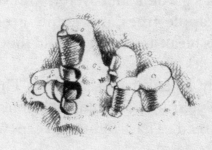

Nine

Smoky saw two surprised faces peering in at him. He opened his mouth in a great big yawn. Then he stood and arched his back, rousing himself from sleep.

For the first time ever, Mandy wasn't glad to see him. In fact, her heart gave a thud of disappointment. As Smoky leaped from his chair and came padding across the carpet towards them, tail up, ready to say hello, she turned away.

'No, wait a minute . . .' James chewed his lip. 'Maybe Smoky can help us!'

Mandy didn't see how. She stood on the patio, trying to get over this latest disappointment.

Grandad's garden, all covered with snow, with its bare apple trees and empty greenhouse, looked as bleak as she felt. Would they ever find Amber?

'Mandy, listen!' James insisted. 'This garden is Smoky's territory. He thinks it belongs to him.'

She agreed. 'That's right. He keeps watch over it.'

'Just like Eric at home. He has a track that he follows, like the one by the fence. He kind of travels a network of paths on his home patch.' He knew that male cats were especially keen to keep invaders out.

Mandy began to see what he was getting at. 'So, if there's another cat around, Smoky would soon see him off.'

'Or *her*!' James suggested. He stared through the glass door at Smoky, who miaowed silently to be let out.

'You mean, if Amber is anywhere round here, Smoky would soon find out?'

James nodded. His eyes were wide with excitement behind his round glasses. 'What do you think?'

'It's worth a try!' Immediately Mandy seized the handle and slid the door open for Smoky to step out. 'Come on, Smoky. There's a good cat.' She stopped to stroke him and let him rub against her leg. He trod delicately into the snow, lifted one front paw and shook it.

James eased the door closed behind him. 'Just in case he prefers to run back inside into the warmth!' he whispered.

Smoky raised his head and looked around at the strange white world. His ears twitched and he followed the flight of a sparrow from Grandad's fence to the apple-tree. He flicked his tail and miaowed.

Mandy and James held their breath. They watched Smoky stalk towards the tree. He crouched by the gnarled trunk, staring up at the sparrow. The bird hopped and twittered in the branches above. As Smoky sprang for the trunk and his claws dug into the bark, the sparrow fluttered and flew off. Smoky dropped silently to the ground, disappointed.

When cats chased birds, they were like tigers, Mandy thought. Or like jaguars stalking through the jungle. Smoky settled low on the ground, haunches raised, tail flicking to and fro.

'What's he seen now?' James breathed. They didn't dare move, as Smoky marked out his territory and went prowling down the garden between the rows of snow-covered vegetables.

'Shh!' Mandy crept quietly after the cat. Smoky had picked up a scent. He padded round the water butt, set off on his track by the fence, sniffed again, then turned back in his tracks. He trotted smartly towards the greenhouse, stopped by a half-buried stack of upturned plant-pots and hissed.

They heard a tiny noise; a faint, frightened miaow. The fur rose along Smoky's back as he arched and let out a loud yowl. Mandy and James ran for the greenhouse as fast as their legs would carry them.

Yet, when they got there, expecting to find Amber cowering in a corner, there was only Smoky. He hissed and growled; the fur on his back standing on end as he arched and spat.

'Let's look inside the greenhouse!' Mandy dived for the door. She wrenched it open and peered inside. Empty shelves, empty plant-pots and trays. No kitten.

'Out here!' James listened again and traced the feeble miaow to the row of upturned pots. Some had toppled sideways and lay higgledy-piggledy round the back of the greenhouse.

They were heavy clay pots, big enough for a kitten to get trapped inside . . .

Mandy rushed to help. The faint pleas grew louder. Smoky backed off. He sensed danger and crept to the edge of the vegetable patch, where he crouched, growling steadily.

'She must be stuck under one of these pots!' James tried to reach down the narrow gap between the greenhouse and a tall fence. He overbalanced and fell against the glass panes. The whole greenhouse shook, but nothing broke. Instead, there was the sliding, rushing sound of heavy snow gliding down a smooth slope.

Mandy glanced up at the greenhouse roof. An avalanche of snow hung over the edge; a huge weight of snow just above James's head. 'Watch out!' She darted to pull him clear.

Just in time; the snow inched down the roof, hung for a second, then plunged to the ground in a shuddering thud. The kitten's cries were drowned as a mountain of snow buried her alive.

Gran and Grandad Hope came rushing from the front of the house. 'What was that?' Grandad had heard the noise. He stared in dismay at the solid mass of snow.

'Oh quick!' Mandy cried. 'Amber is under there! We heard her, then the snow fell on top of her. We need a spade to dig her out!'

In a flash Grandad headed for his garden shed. Gran rushed into the house to fetch the fireside shovel. Meanwhile, Mandy and James kneeled to scrape at the pile of snow. There was no sign of Smoky; he had fled across the garden in the rumble of falling snow.

Mandy dug with her bare hands. 'What if she's been crushed?' The snow was heavy, packed into the gap between the fence and the greenhouse. It was about a metre deep.

'Don't think about it!' James scrabbled through the heap.

Soon Grandad came back with his spade. 'Try this!' He handed it to Mandy over James's head. She began to dig.

'Careful!' Gran warned. She gave the smaller shovel to James. He worked at the bottom of the pile, going in sideways.

At last Mandy's spade hit something solid. She scraped at the snow to reveal a cracked plant-pot, tumbled sideways under the avalanche. Digging carefully round it, she pulled it free.

'What's under there?' Grandad craned to see.

'More pots.' Mandy put the spade down and began to scoop with her hands again, while James dug his tunnel through the base of the pile.

'We've got to get air in there!' he gasped, his face red with the effort. 'Amber has to breathe!'

'Perhaps she's trapped under a pot, in a pocket of air,' Gran whispered.

'I hope you're right,' Grandad murmured.

Mandy pulled a second pot from the heap. It was broken in two. She thought she heard a faint cry from deep in the snow. Her heart leaped. 'Did you hear that?' In a frenzy she scraped at the snow, digging deeper and deeper.

'Yes!' James stopped tunnelling to listen. 'I heard it!'

'Oh be careful, Mandy!' Gran repeated. Any second the pile of snow could collapse and crush the kitten to death.

Mandy lifted out another shard of broken pot. The snow shifted and slid. She stopped, gathered her nerve and began again. This time she brought out a whole plant-pot, then another.

The cries grew louder, more insistent: *Miaow . . . miaow . . . miaow!*

Mandy scraped at the snow. She uncovered a pot. It was turned upside-down, like part of a giant sandcastle made of snow. She did more careful scraping. The pot tilted then jolted back into position. The kitten wailed, then went quiet again.

'Ready?' Mandy breathed. She seized the pot with both hands, fingers frozen, arms trembling. She lifted it inch by inch so that the surrounding snow stayed in place. And there, under the plant-pot, hunched in a bedraggled ball, her orange eyes staring up at them, was Amber!

* * *

The news spread down the lane like wildfire; Mandy and James had found the kitten. Ernie, Brandon, Susan and Mr Hastings came running to Lilac Cottage. Mrs Ponsonby went to the village to proclaim the good tidings. Walter called in at Animal Ark to tell the Hopes. Soon everyone knew.

By this time Mandy had carried Amber into the house. She asked her gran for a towel and began to rub the kitten dry. Amber shivered and huddled inside the towel, mewing quietly.

'What about a hot-water bottle?' Grandad asked. They were still worried about hypothermia.

'No, she shouldn't have direct heat,' Mandy said. 'We mustn't warm her up too quickly. We just have to get her dry.' She said she didn't think there were any broken bones, but that Amber might have frostbite; she couldn't tell yet.

'Can she have warm milk?' Gran asked. They stood peering over James's head at Mandy kneeling in the kitchen floor with the kitten on her lap.

Mandy nodded. Soon Amber's fur was dry and fluffy. Gran brought a saucer of milk and Mandy set her gently on her feet. The kitten wobbled, then stooped to lap with her pink tongue. Mandy rested back on her heels and looked up at the worried faces. Her wet blonde hair was streaked across her cheek and neck. Her skin still tingled with cold. 'I think she's going to be all right!' she whispered.

A crowd had gathered outside the gate as Mandy wrapped Amber in a thick red blanket and took her out to Grandad's camper-van. They planned to drive to Beechtrees to deliver the kitten safely back home.

'Well done!'

'Isn't that great!'

'Oh, she's gorgeous!' There was a general murmur of approval at the sight of the rescued kitten.

Mandy let the helpers have a peep. There Amber sat, warmly wrapped up, purring like a little engine. She peered out from the red blanket at the row of strange faces, gave a puzzled miaow and snuggled deeper into Mandy's arms.

Grandad thanked everyone as he opened the gate. 'All's well that ends well!' He smiled and went to wait in the van.

Gran beckoned from the doorstep. 'Come on, Mandy. Don't keep that poor little girl waiting a moment longer!' She went to wave them off through the gate.

Mandy sat in the front with Amber, James in the back. Mr Hastings climbed in too, then slid the door of the camper-van shut.

They were on their way at last to give Amber back to Alex.

'Just in time,' Jeremy Hastings murmured. He stared out of the window across the valley at the twinkling lights of Welford village.

Just in time for Christmas, just in time for the grand procession; above all, just in time for Alex.

Mandy took Amber into Alex's bedroom. The kitten was still wrapped in the red woollen blanket. 'Look who I've brought,' she whispered.

Alex was still in bed, staring at the ceiling. Her hair shone coppery-red against the white pillows. She turned her head, hardly daring to believe her eyes.

Mandy tiptoed forward. 'It's Amber!'

'Really and truly?' Alex propped herself on her elbows. Then she sat up. 'Let me see!'

She unwrapped the blanket. Amber's round face peered out, eyes alert as she recognised the room. She sprang from Mandy's arms on to the bed, and went padding softly towards Alex.

The little girl held her arms wide open. She was speechless with delight. Amber stole straight into her arms. Alex wrapped them around the kitten, put her cheek against Amber's soft head and looked up at Mandy. 'Did Father Christmas tell you where to look?'

Mandy smiled. Alex's dream had come true. No more worries, no more tears. Now she could concentrate on getting better. 'In a way, yes I suppose he did,' she said.

Ten

Don McNab was polite about Gran's specially made Father Christmas outfit. 'It's very good of you to go to all this trouble,' he said as she brought it into the yard at Animal Ark. He was busy transforming the trailer into the reindeer sleigh. 'But the old gentleman won't be needing it after all!'

Mandy and James were helping Don. It was seven o'clock; they had just half an hour to get the sleigh ready and to harness Rudolph and Dasher, before they were due in the village square. The evening was crisp and clear, a perfect Christmas Eve.

'Are you sure?' Gran was puzzled. As far as she knew, Don had left the proper outfit stranded in a hospital ward.

'Quite sure, thank you. I got a message to Father Christmas and he had a spare one specially sent down from Reindeerland!'

'Ah well.' She raised her eyebrows, then tucked the home-made suit back into her carrier bag. 'Perhaps it will come in useful another year.' Intrigued by the sleigh, she walked right round it. She admired the fibreglass side panels as James bolted them into place, and inspected the bulky pile of presents in the back. 'Lovely!' she told Mandy. 'I may be an old lady, but I confess I'm very excited!'

Mandy nodded. 'I know. I can hardly wait.'

'They're ready for you in the square,' Gran told Don. 'The fairy lights look beautiful. They've hung huge, old-fashioned lanterns outside the pub. And the music is already playing.'

'Is there anyone there yet?' Mandy asked. All they needed now for the procession to be a success was a huge crowd of people singing carols, all gathered to see Father Christmas and his sleigh.

'Quite a few. Your grandad and I are on our

way back there now. Would you like a lift?'

But Mandy and James weren't quite ready. 'No thanks. We'll come down with Mum. Dad's had to go out on a call, so we'll meet him there.' She wanted to help Don hitch Rudolph and Dasher to the sleigh before they set off for the village.

So Gran said she would see him later. 'Don't be too long,' she warned, 'or you'll miss all the fun!'

But Mandy and James couldn't think of anything better than helping with the reindeer. They went to lead them out of the compound, smartly groomed, hooves clicking, white manes fluffed out. Their velvety antlers cast wonderful shadows across the yard.

'That's right, steady on!' Don encouraged as they entered them in between the shafts of the sleigh. 'Come on now, Dasher, back a wee bit further! That's it, Rudolph, you show him how it's done!' Slowly they eased the reindeer into position.

Dasher grunted and pawed the ground. The sleigh shifted behind him. Rudolph stood, the picture of patience, as if he sensed that their big moment had come.

'Grand!' Don was satisfied at last.

They stood back for the full effect. It was as good as they could possibly imagine; a gleaming sleigh with polished white sides, decorated in red and gold. There was a pile of presents stacked high on top, and two beautiful reindeer to draw it along the snowy lane. James glanced at Mandy, stuck both hands deep in his pockets, and raised his shoulders in a contented sigh.

'Right, you two!' Emily Hope called from the drive. 'We haven't got much time. I'll race you there!'

Mandy grinned. Her mum was dressed in a brown velvet hat with a fake-fur brim, a long, dark Russian-style coat and long boots. She looked too smart to race, Mandy thought. 'Can't we wait for Don?' she pleaded.

'No!' came the instant reply. Don was still busy checking the harness. 'Father Christmas doesn't like having folk around when he gets here. He's a wee bit on the shy side, like young James there!' He winked, and James blushed. 'You go on ahead,' he told them. 'Go and enjoy yourselves!'

So they had to say goodbye for now to Rudolph and Dasher.

'Twenty minutes to go,' Mandy's mum said as they set off on foot.

'I hope Dad gets back in time,' Mandy said. As luck would have it, the phone had rung and he'd had to go out. 'A vet's life,' he'd sighed. 'Always on call, always having to go and tend the sick and wounded!'

'Aah!' they'd cried. Mandy and James had felt truly sorry for him.

'Take no notice,' Emily Hope had told them. 'He's only playing for sympathy!'

So now they walked quickly along the lane in a threesome; Mandy, James and Mrs Hope. As they drew near the main street, they saw a string of parked cars, and heard carols playing over the loudspeakers. Then they saw the square. It basked in a glow of lights; yellow, red and green. A giant Christmas tree stood proudly in the middle, all lit up. A huge crowd was gathered round it.

Mandy felt a thrill of excitement. There were children running around, or perched on grown-ups' shoulders. There was Walter leaning on his garden gate, watching events, the Parker Smythes standing with Sam Western. Simon was talking to Jean, and Sara Hardy was dressed up in Victorian costume, wearing a long, hooped skirt and a shawl, taking round big trays of mince-pies.

Then Julian Hardy came out of the pub to conduct the singing. He handed out carol sheets. Everyone stood ready.

'There are hundreds of people here!' James tried to count, but gave up.

Mandy smiled at her mum, then slid in among the crowd. She took a song-sheet, on the look-out for her father, but instead she spied Gran and Grandad. They gave her a wave. She waved back, continuing to thread her way towards the front.

> '*While shepherds watched their flocks*
> *by night,*
> *All seated on the ground,*
> *The angel of the Lord came down,*
> *And glory shone around!*'

Faces in the crowded square were lit by lantern light. They opened their mouths and sang. The music floated into the night sky, a chorus of happy voices.

> '*Away in a-a man-ger,*
> *No-o crib for a bed . . .*'

Mandy sang her heart out. But where was her dad?

Surely he should have finished his call by now. She edged sideways out of the crowd, to look down the road for the Animal Ark Land-rover.

But there, by the side of the Fox and Goose, she was waylaid by the strange sight of two Father Christmases arguing.

'Aye well, when I heard they were short of someone to do the job, I thought I'd better step in.' A grumpy voice growled from behind a fake white beard. The figure was hidden behind a red hood and cloak, but Ernie's trousers and sturdy boots were unmistakeable.

'Yes, and that was very kind of you!'

Mandy opened her eyes wide. Here too was a voice she recognised.

'It was really very thoughtful, Mr Bell. But now I think you should leave it all to me!'

This figure was short and round, with a big chest beneath the red, fur-trimmed coat. The hood was pulled well up, and the fruity voice muffled behind an outsize white beard. But it was true; Mrs Ponsonby was taking charge as usual. 'I know how to deal with small children, you see. You might frighten the poor little things. Now step aside and let me pass. We mustn't disappoint our public, must we?'

Ernie chuntered and grumbled. He wasn't going to give in without a fight. 'Look here, I had to borrow this lot from the wardrobe department at the Welford Players. They didn't let me have it for nothing neither!'

Mrs Ponsonby eyed the moth-eaten costume as if to say that Ernie had been robbed. She smoothed her own posh costume and stroked her beard. Mandy choked back a laugh.

'Break it up there!' Julian Hardy stepped in with a smile between the two would-be Father Christmases. The carols soared on. No one except Mandy had seen or heard the squabble. 'Didn't you hear? The real Father Christmas got back safely after all!'

'Surely not?'

'Well, I never!' Mrs Ponsonby and Ernie were stunned into silence. They unhooked their beards and threw back their hoods in the shadow of the pub wall. Suddenly the music changed. Bells jingled through the loudspeakers. All the children squeezed to the very front and peered up the street.

A roar of voices struck up with the first lines of Rudolph's song as Father Christmas's sleigh came into sight.

It was magical. Rudolph and Dasher pranced towards the square. The sleigh was all lit up with tiny white lights, silver bells jangled; it shone and sparkled as the reindeer drew near.

'Father Christmas!' the small ones gasped.

'Is he real?'

'Oh look, it's Rudolph!'

They all looked on in wonder.

Father Christmas sat up high, holding the reins; a round man with a red face and a big white beard. He was quite the most believable Father Christmas Mandy had ever seen.

Mandy felt James creep up alongside her. 'Doesn't Don look great?' she said.

'Shh!' He glanced round to make sure that no one had heard. 'Don't spoil it!'

They grinned at each other. Don McNab certainly looked realistic as he stopped the sleigh in the square and stepped down. His loud voice boomed out a great 'Ho-ho-ho!'

'What do you think to him?' a voice asked quietly over their shoulders. 'The gentleman got here on time, just like I promised.' The voice had a definite Scottish accent.

'Don!' Mandy and James jumped sky-high.

'But you're . . .'

'You should be up . . .'

They stopped dead. Don grinned back. He stood there large as life in his thick jumper and jacket. 'Och no,' he protested. 'You didn't still think *I* was the old man! Do you not believe in the real Father Christmas, after all I've told you?'

They gulped.

'They do now.' Emily smiled as she passed by with a collection-box. She shook it in time to the tune. People reached deep in their pockets and gave generously. They said it was the best Christmas sleigh they'd ever seen.

When Mandy and James turned again to quiz Don, the Scotsman had melted away into the crowd.

Then there were gifts for the small children. They went up shyly one by one to whisper their Christmas wish. Father Christmas delved into the pile of wrapped presents and found the right sort. The child went off hugging the parcel while mums and dads added money to the collection-boxes. The queue seemed to go on for ever, as kids with shining eyes got to stroke Father Christmas's reindeer.

At last all the carols had been sung, the presents given out. Collectors returned to the pub with their tins, where Gran and Grandad Hope counted up the total. More mince-pies were eaten, and then the crowd lined up along the street, ready for Father Christmas's sleigh to move on towards Beechtrees.

'He's due to make a special stop,' Mandy's mum explained. She stood between Mandy and James, waiting to hear Grandad's announcement of the grand total.

Grandad climbed on to the sleigh, sheet of paper in hand. He asked for quiet. The music faded, the excited voices died. Clearing his throat, he read from the paper. 'We have collected a grand total of eight hundred and seventy nine pounds and thirty pence!' he announced proudly. 'Which, I'm delighted to say, means Alex and her family will be off to the States as soon as possible in the New Year! Well done, everyone, and thank you very much!'

Grandad got down from the sleigh to a round of applause. Then the crowd formed a long procession behind the sleigh.

'Come on.' Emily Hope put an arm round Mandy and James's shoulders. 'We can't miss the best bit!' She led them into the procession. They walked slowly to the jingle of bells and the click of the reindeer's hooves.

Before they knew it, they were outside the bungalow, underneath the tall trees. Father Christmas drew the reindeer to a halt. 'Ho-ho-ho!' he greeted the people at the house.

William appeared at the front window. He pulled back the curtain, gasped, then shot off. Soon the door opened and he stood in the porch, eyes bright, as Father Christmas beckoned him.

'Go on, William!' Mrs Hastings appeared behind her son and whispered softly. She put a hand on his shoulder and nudged him down the step. He ran down the path, shook hands with the figure in red and took a huge present from him. His mum stood by, smiling.

'Say thank you,' she prompted.

William could hardly see over his mysterious box. 'Thank you!' he whispered.

'And thank you, from Alex's dad and me too,' Mrs Hastings told Mandy. 'Your grandad tells me we can all go to America for Alex's operation.' Quickly she brushed a tear away as Jeremy Hastings hurried inside to fetch their daughter. She took Mandy in her arms and gave her a great big hug.

And now it was Alex's turn. She came to the step with her dad, all wrapped up in coat, scarf and hat, carrying Amber. The kitten blinked at the lights on the sleigh.

'Here, give her to me,' Mr Hastings urged Alex.

As if in a daze, she handed Amber over and came slowly down the path. Father Christmas welcomed her with open arms. She smiled up at him; a dazzling, disbelieving smile. Then he lifted her clean off her feet and into the sleigh.

'Choose a present!' he boomed.

Alex pointed shyly to a small, round parcel. All the people who had helped to make this the best Christmas ever looked on, as she tore off the wrapping. Inside was a tiny blue leather collar with a silver bell. She held it up to show Mandy. 'Look! He must have got the letter. He brought this for Amber!'

Her dad came forward with a smile and handed her the kitten. Carefully Alex fitted the collar around Amber's neck.

'Would you like a ride?' Father Christmas let her and the kitten snuggle up close.

Wide-eyed, she stared up at him and nodded. 'Can William come too?'

'Plenty of room!' Father Christmas replied.

No sooner said than done, Jeremy Hastings hoisted his son up on to the sleigh.

Then Father Christmas took up the reins. 'Gee up, Rudolph! Gee up, Dasher!' The reindeer jerked once, then they were smoothly in step, clicking down the road.

Mandy and James ran to keep up. Behind them, the crowd struck up another verse from 'Rudolph'.

Father Christmas joined in the song as he drove his sleigh along the snowy road. His deep voice boom-boomed through the clear night air.

Mandy and James stopped dead.

'You don't think . . . ?' James stared and stammered.

Mandy swallowed hard. 'No!' Father Christmas was fat and jolly, his beard was white. Her dad's was brown. 'Then again, where *is* Dad right this minute?'

They watched as the sleigh turned and came back towards them.

'Magnificent, eh?'

Mandy whirled round at the sound of the familiar deep voice. 'Dad!' He stood behind them, wrapped in scarf and hat.

'What's wrong? I said I'd be back in time for the celebrations, didn't I?'

'B-but!' She gazed again at the splendid red figure on the sleigh.

Adam Hope smiled broadly, and clapped his gloved hands. 'Merry Christmas!' he shouted above the jingling bells.

The sleigh drew up beside them, the reindeer grunted and shook their harnesses. Alex held tight to her kitten. She and William beamed at them. Then Mr Hastings came and lifted the children down to the ground.

Finally, the old gentleman looked Mandy and James straight in the eye. He gave one of his booming ho-ho-ho laughs. 'Merry Christmas!' he said. They waved up at him, as he took the reins and drove off. 'Merry Christmas, everyone!'

Read more about Animal Ark in
Puppies in Trouble

One

'What *is* that smell?' asked Mandy Hope as she walked through the door from her home into the reception at Animal Ark. She wrinkled her nose. 'It smells like a hairdresser's in here!'

Jean Knox, the surgery receptionist, put a finger to her lips. Then, she chuckled. 'It's Toby. I think Mrs Ponsonby has drenched him in her perfume. Apparently he found something rather nasty to roll in – and came home smelling bad enough to cause Pandora to have a fit!'

'Oh no!' Mandy said, grinning. Everyone in Welford knew what a fuss-pot Mrs Ponsonby was where the little Pekinese was concerned.

'Not a real fit?' she whispered.

Jean grinned and shrugged her shoulders. She put on her glasses and went back to the paperwork on her desk.

Mandy looked over the counter to where Mrs Ponsonby was sitting in the surgery waiting-room. Apart from the stout, smartly dressed lady and her two dogs, the waiting-room was empty. The surgery was unusually quiet for a Saturday morning.

Mrs Ponsonby was wafting a lace-edged handkerchief under her nose with one hand and holding her scruffy mongrel pup, Toby, on the lead with the other. Pandora, the Pekinese, sat on Mrs Ponsonby's lap, her long creamy-coloured fur spread out over her owner's flowery dress. The spoilt little dog looked calm and untroubled.

'Hello, Mrs Ponsonby,' Mandy called.

'Mandy, dear!' breathed Mrs Ponsonby, looking up. 'Have you any idea just how much longer your father is likely to be? Only, I rather think this is an emergency visit . . .'

'He's in the middle of an operation, Mrs Ponsonby, but Mrs Hope shouldn't be much longer,' Jean called. 'And there's no one ahead of you in the queue today, so you should be able to go straight in, in a minute or two.'

'Yes,' Mandy said reassuringly. 'It's really quiet for a Saturday morning surgery.'

She slipped out from behind the reception desk and went to say hello to Toby and Pandora. 'What's Pandora's problem, Mrs Ponsonby?' she asked.

'Well,' said Mrs Ponsonby, looking pained, 'Toby arrived in the kitchen this morning reeking of something foul, which upset poor Pandora. I'm certain she had a fit of some kind. She was panting, and her eyes were bulging – it was awful. And then I decided to disguise the dreadful smell with some perfume, but I splashed it in Toby's eye and he gave such a terrible yell . . .'

Mandy noticed that one of Toby's eyes was half-closed, but he seemed to be in his usual high spirits. He wagged his tail happily at Mandy. She stroked his head. The scent of lavender, mingling with the more pungent stench that Toby had so happily rolled in, rose into the air. Mandy coughed. 'Never mind, Toby,' she said. 'We'll have you back to normal in no time. Both of you,' she added, smiling at Pandora. 'Sounds like you've had a bad morning, Mrs Ponsonby.'

'I have, dear,' Mrs Ponsonby sighed.

As Mandy was fussing Toby, the door of one of the treatment rooms opened. She turned round and saw her mother washing her hands at the basin. A man holding a cat in a wicker basket was just leaving the treatment room. 'Thanks so much,' he said. 'I'll bring Cassie back in a day or two. Goodbye.'

'Bye,' said Mrs Hope, drying her hands on a small towel. Toby yapped sharply as the cat let out a mournful wail.

Mandy's mother waved at her through the open door of the treatment room, then spotted Mrs Ponsonby, who was struggling to stand up with Pandora in her arms.

'Hello, Mrs Ponsonby,' Mrs Hope called cheerfully, tucking a few strands of her long red hair behind her ear. 'Come along in. Oh . . . both of them today, is it?' She winked at Mandy, then closed the door.

Jean caught Mandy's eye and they laughed. Mandy wandered over to the window. It was a hot July day, and the green hills beyond the village looked inviting in the sunshine.

It wouldn't be long until the start of the school summer holidays, she thought happily. There would be lots of opportunities to help out at Animal Ark once school was finished, and hours of exploring the hills around Welford with her best friend James Hunter and his Labrador, Blackie.

'Ah, here comes a patient!' Mandy told Jean, who was busy with some paperwork. Mandy went to open the surgery door for a visitor she hadn't seen before. He was a tall, tanned man dressed in a blue denim shirt and jeans, and carrying a large cardboard box against his chest. He smiled as Mandy stood aside to let him in.

'Mr Taylor,' he told Jean, propping the edge of the box on the counter. 'And this is Rush. He's come for his twelve-week vaccination.'

'Hello,' Jean smiled. 'Would you just fill out this card for me, please, Mr Taylor? Mr Hope is just finishing a small operation. We won't keep you long.'

'May I see Rush?' Mandy asked Mr Taylor, pointing to the box.

Animal Ark™

**For more information about
Animal Ark and for the latest news
on the books and how you can
get involved, visit the website:**

www.animalark.co.uk

*Hodder
Children's
Books*

A division of Hachette Children's Books